Sticks -n- Stones

& A BAG OF BONES

Written by Laurie Moran and Amber Newberry

Illustrated by Linden Walker

Edited by Jacqueline Brousseau

FOR THE STRANGE KIDS:

WEIRD IS A GOOD THING

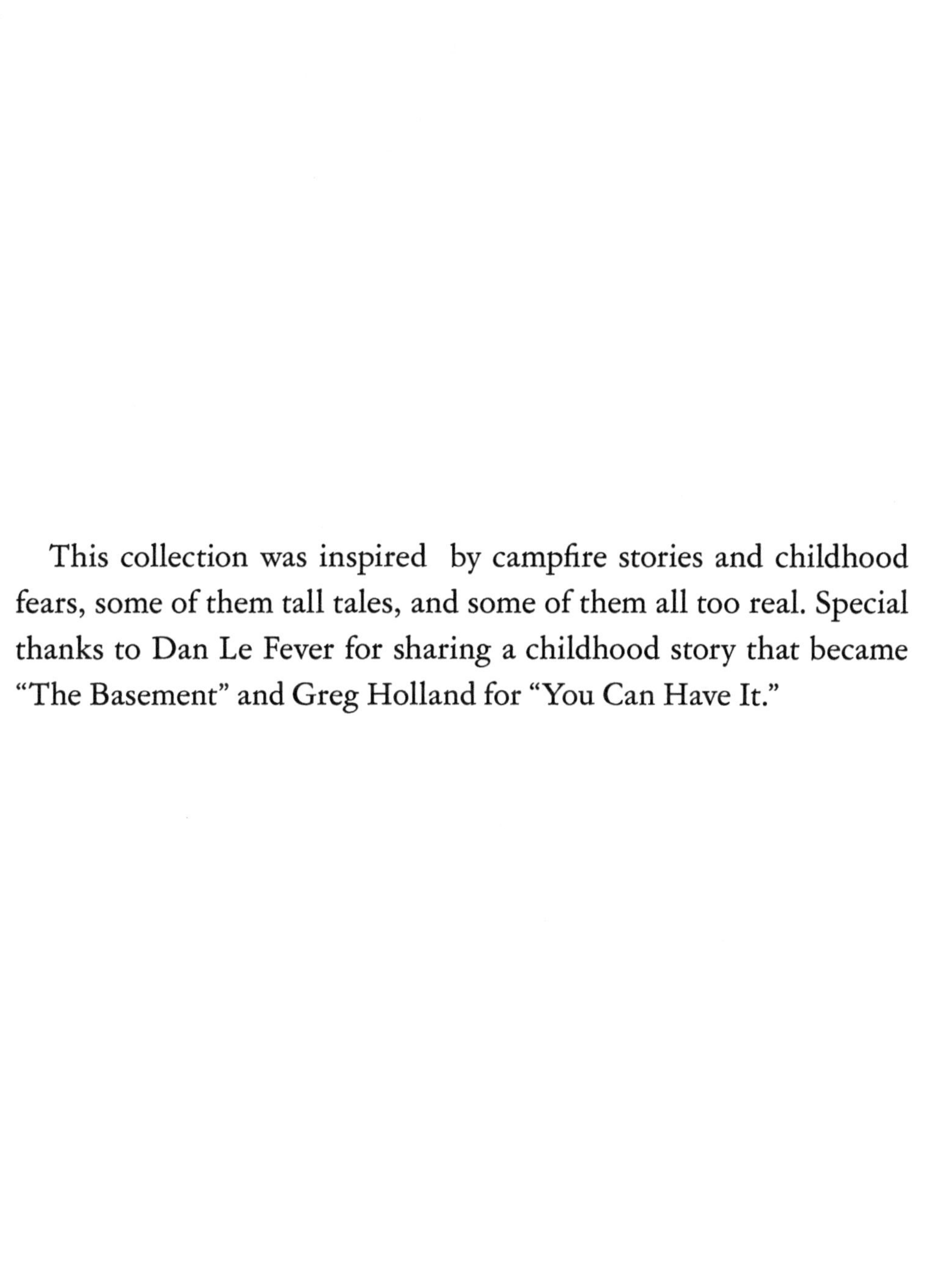

This collection was inspired by campfire stories and childhood fears, some of them tall tales, and some of them all too real. Special thanks to Dan Le Fever for sharing a childhood story that became "The Basement" and Greg Holland for "You Can Have It."

TABLE OF CONTENTS

GHASTLY GHOSTS, MACABRE MONSTERS, AND BONE-CHILLING... BUGS?

Bag of Bones ...11

Fly Trap ...27

Camp Carpenter ...33

Job Vacancy ...39

The Pier ...45

You Can Have It ...51

The Abominable Grumbalo ...57

Apparitions ...65

The Eguh Rets Nom ...70

A Portrait of Betsy ...73

Meg Looked Up ...81

The Basement ...89

Closet Monsters ...95

TABLE OF CONTENTS

THERE'S SOMETHING NOT QUITE RIGHT ABOUT THAT THING

A Driving Lesson ...103

GameStation VK ...107

The Tree ...113

The Reflection ...117

The Book ...121

A WORD OF ADVICE

The Gluttonous Thief ...127

The Starling ...131

Eli Was A Dead Man ...135

The Necklace ...139

Hold Your Breath ...145

The Photo Album ...151

Snake Oil ...157

Sticks n Stones ...165

The Marble Garden ...171

THE CAMPFIRE

GHASTLY GHOSTS, MACABRE MONSTERS, & BONE-CHILLING... BUGS?

BAG OF BONES

"Hey Damien, come over here and look what I found!" Dorian called out to her twin brother.

Damien dodged the trees of Salem Woods heading in the direction of his sister's voice. They often broke up their walk home from school by taking the long way through the woods, half to push off having to do homework a little longer, and half for the various treasures they'd find there. Damien had a pocket full of small rocks and other objects he'd found on the forest floor, and it had a musical rhythm to it as he jogged along, expertly leaping over roots and uneven earth. Freshly fallen leaves in autumnal hues layered the path and crunched under his second-hand combat boots. Both twins knew this part of the woods well, a short way from the well-trodden trails that were more heavily populated with hikers.

Damien came to a denser part of the woods where the trees were thicker and still heavily covered in the colorful leaves of October, he saw his sister kneeling over something he couldn't quite make out until he got closer.

"What is it?" Damien asked as he crouched down for a closer look. It was an old burlap bag; crumbled clots of dried mud shook off it as Dorian pulled apart the opening at the top to reveal a pile of bones.

"Oh man, that's so cool!" Damien said, reaching out for one of the relics. Dorian's hand flew up, blocking her brother from touching the bones.

"What if there's rabies, or something?" Dorian warned her brother.

"Don't be stupid, there's no flesh left. It's just bone!" Damien said, again reaching for one of the pieces. He retrieved a long, white portion from the sack and examined it closely. Dorian rolled her eyes at her brother and reached out and gingerly picked a bone from the pile. She'd wanted to make sure the bones stayed intact, in case they were important, but since Damien had already touched one, she thought it probably wouldn't matter if she also examined just one.

"What kinda animal do you think this was?" Damien asked, grabbing the bag and dumping it out onto the ground.

"I don't know, could all be from different things," Dorian replied, exasperated by her brother's lack of care. As the pile was disturbed, Dorian noticed a piece she wanted to inspect closer. She reached into the pile and pulled out a jaw, several teeth still attached. "This isn't an animal, that's human! Look!" Dorian held it up, allowing it to catch what little of the afternoon light still shone through the branches of the trees.

"How do you know that?" Damien asked.

"Are you kidding? Look at the shape! Didn't we just take a test on anatomy like a month ago?" Dorian reminded him, pride apparent in her tone. It was one of the few things she'd been really interested in learning about in their Biology class, though she was at a loss for the scientific name. "It's the jawbone!"

"The mandible," Damien corrected his twin smugly.

"Yeah, the mandible," Dorian said flatly. Her brother might have been better with vocabulary, but at least Dorian knew it was human just by looking at it.

The pair looked at the pearly whites all in a row with awe. Damien thought of what the bones would look like spread out on a table or wired up in order, the way the plastic one was in Mrs. Bundy's classroom. 'Articulated' she'd told him when he'd asked about it. Dorian thought of the person the bones might have belonged to.

That's when the 'twin thing' caught up to them and their thoughts seemed to hit all the same realizations at exactly the same moment.

How long ago did they die?

How did they die?

Why were they discarded like this?

They turned to look each other in the eye, the panic finally hitting them.

"We've got to tell someone," Dorian said.

"Yeah, we've got to tell someone," Damien agreed.

"We could call the cops," Dorian suggested.

"I hate cops," Damien said.

"Me too." Dorian pulled out her phone and held it up. It was dead. "No juice."

"Mom took mine away and still hasn't given it back."

"You just had to do that idiotic surf challenge."

"It would've been fine if I didn't get caught before posting the video."

"She still would've grounded you when she saw it."

"But at least it would've gotten posted before she took my phone."

"And mom's car wouldn't be in the shop."

"Ok, but it was just a little scratch." Damien shrugged.

"Either way," Dorian said, "I don't want the cops jumping to conclusions getting a call from us so soon after—"

"The incident?" Damien interrupted, laughing.

"The incident," Dorian also laughed.

"You're right, though," Damien said. "That one officer has it out for us ever since last summer."

"Excuse me?" Dorian asked. "Are you blaming your problem with that cop on my kissing his daughter last summer?"

"I'm not, not saying that," Damien gave his sister a gentle push.

"Okay," she admitted, "you might not be wrong about that, but we broke up months ago."

"I'm just saying," Damien teased.

"We can call in an anonymous tip," Dorian suggested, wanting to get back to the issue at hand.

"I don't think we should just leave them here," Damien said.

"Oh no, we're not bringing that home with us. Mom would kill us," Dorian replied.

"It's starting to get dark. Mom's going to be mad if we aren't back before it gets dark. What if we just bring them home with us tonight? We'll hide them and take them down to the police station early tomorrow morning and leave them outside. They'll know what to do and don't have to know it was us," Damien said.

"I don't know... all of those police shows always say to leave a body where you found it," Dorian argued.

"It's not a body... anymore," Damien leveled. "And besides, if we leave the bones here someone might take them, or what if we can't find them again?"

"Alright," Dorian agreed. "Just for tonight, then I'll take them to the cops tomorrow to keep you off their radar."

The twins carried the sack of bones out of the woods to where they'd left their bikes. They rode home and quickly ran up the stairs

to their bedrooms, where they placed the burlap bag in their old toy chest in the hallway and covered it with a sheet.

"Good thing mom made us donate all our old toys over the summer," Dorian said as she closed the lid.

"Imagine if mom looked in there and found it full of bones," Damien laughed nervously.

"I'd be fine," Doran shrugged. "You're the one always getting into trouble."

"Yes, but it's always the quiet nerdy people you'd least expect who turn out to be murderers," Damien countered.

"Shut it!" Dorian laughed as she pushed past him. "Let's eat." He followed her down the stairs.

When they finished their dinner and homework, they escaped to an early bedtime under the pretense that they were tired and had a test the next day. Once the two thought their parents believed them to be asleep, they quietly dragged out the bag of bones and began examining each piece, comparing it to the diagram in a biology textbook on the floor of Damien's room they used to share when they were little.

"I've got the thorax," Dorian said.

"Thorax. That sounds like a name for a dinosaur… or one of those bad '80s heavy metal bands," Damien joked as he got up to open his windows. It was unseasonably warm all day and the evening was finally cool enough to enjoy.

"Don't forget to close that one," Dorian reminded him as he opened the one without a screen. It let out onto the top of the porch, and they had removed the screen so they could sneak out and watch the stars from the roof. "Mom will kill you if the house is filled with flies tomorrow."

"Noted," Damien said.

The pair laid out each bone until it resembled the diagram. A twin stood on either side and stared down at the skeleton. Neither had been truly disturbed by what they'd found until that moment—the moment it started to really look like a person.

"We should've left it out there," Dorian said. Damien didn't disagree.

"Let's get him—I mean it—back into the bag," Damien said.

They gently placed each piece back into the burlap sack and put the skull on the very top before covering it back up with the sheet in the toy chest. Each twin lay quietly in their beds in their own rooms, unable to get the skeleton out of their thoughts. They often slept with their doors open so they could talk. It was a long time before they began to fall asleep, but before they could, they began to hear what sounded like a rattling in the hallway.

"Dorian, do you hear that?" Damien asked quietly.

"Yeah," Dorian said as she shot up and turned on the lamp in her room. The noise stopped. Both of them stared into the darkness of the hallway between them.

"It wasn't my imagination if we both heard it, right?" Damien asked, getting up and walking to the doorway.

"I don't know," Dorian replied, standing up.

"How do you not know? You heard it, it scared the crap out of you. You're the one who turned a light on," Damien argued.

"Yeah, but you would've turned yours on a second later," Dorian responded.

"You've always been afraid of the dark!" Damien shot back.

"Go back to sleep!" Their mom called from downstairs.

"I have not, now go back to sleep. We're just creeping ourselves out," Dorian said. They each went back to their respective beds.

Damien leaned back into his pillows in the darkness of his room. Dorian covered herself up and turned the lamp off in her room. Each twin lay silently in bed, listening. Eventually, they both drifted off to an uneasy sleep.

The twins were jolted awake by a frantic sound in the hallway, as if the lid of the toybox was being pushed up and dropped over and over. The lamp was switched on and as soon as light charged Dorian's room, the sound was gone, as though it had never happened. Dorian had jumped out of her bed and grasped a pillow to her chest. Damien went to the doorway to find his sister staring back at him from her room. He walked into the hallway and turned the main light on. Dorian stayed in her doorway as Damien approached the toy chest.

They each let out a sigh of relief as Damien lifted the lid to reveal nothing out of the ordinary. A sheet covered a lumpy mass that was the bag of bones. The lid creaked as Damien shut it again. Dorian joined him in the hallway and they stared down at the toy chest. It was very old, handmade by their great grandfather for his children. It had been painted a few times over the years and was scratched up and even peeling in several spots. There were applique decals of clowns and circus animals that had been on it since the sixties. It had seen better days, that was certain, and the years of age had made the decorations dingy and warped. One clown had only half a face and a one-legged elephant stood on a platform that was peeling up from the paint. They looked at the closed chest in silence, puzzled.

Finally, they turned to go back to bed, but as soon as their backs turned, they heard a creak, and then a slam!

"Don't pretend you didn't just hear that!" Damien said as they both turned back to face the toy chest.

"I heard it," Dorian replied as she let the pillow drop from her chest. "We should've left it in the woods."

"Them," Damien corrected.

"Them… We should've left 'them' in the woods," Dorian said. Damien didn't argue.

"Well, what do we do, now?" Damien asked.

"Let's go sleep in the living room," Dorian suggested.

"What if we hear that noise again?" Damien asked, after they gathered up their blankets and pillows.

"It probably can't get out, anyway. You can't grab or push anything with just bones," Dorian tried to be logical.

Just to be safe, Damien put a couple of books on top of the toy chest to weigh it down. Then, the twins quietly made their way to the living room where they each sprawled out on part of the huge sectional sofa, their feet meeting at the corner.

This time it was much harder to fall asleep. The twins tried to occupy their minds by talking for a while. Damien had started to fall asleep first and was a deep sleeper, but Dorian lay awake for a long time before she felt her eyelids become heavy. As she began to succumb to sleep, she thought she heard a faint rattling from upstairs. She opened her eyes and tried to listen, but couldn't hear anything. She decided it was just in her head. She tried to relax; it was well past one o'clock in the morning and was tired from the long day. Damien had the benefit of wearing himself out at hockey practice earlier in the day. Dorian had scrolled on her phone waiting for him until it went dead, and now she wished she was more interested in sports because she envied how easily her brother fell into a deep sleep even after everything. Finally, she felt herself drifting off again.

Then there was a definitive thud.

Dorian sat upright and listened.

All was quiet as her eyes adjusted. Dull moonlight allowed her to make out the shape of things in the room: the tv, the hearth, the banister at the end of the staircase.

Then there was a rattling, like a wooden chime blowing in the breeze.

"Damien, are you awake?" Dorian asked. Damien didn't respond.

The sound grew closer, and closer. It began to sound like a wooden chime in a windstorm, Dorian also noticed the sound of fabric moving, like a sheet on a laundry line or curtains at a window left open during a blizzard.

"Damien, wake up," Dorian pleaded, but Damien still lay silently on his section of the couch.

The rattling grew ever closer as goosebumps began to rise on Dorian's arms and neck.

"Damien, please wake up," Dorian begged her brother.

It was then that she saw it: the silhouette of a skeleton, half covered with a sheet that was caught in a phantom breeze. The skull and a shoulder attached to a skeletal arm were all that Dorian could make out in the darkness, the rest of the bones were shadows, covered by the thin, white sheet that hung raggedly over it. The fabric caught the moonlight occasionally as it flapped in a false gust.

"Wha--," Dorian stammered, "what do you want?"

There was a strange, windy moan as it glided closer to where Dorian lay, rattling as it moved. Dorian began to kick at Damien's feet until he finally awoke to see what stood before them.

"How did you—" Damien began, but he lost his words as the skeletal creature crept closer, the moan like a guttural draft blowing through a tunnel.

"What do we do?" Dorian asked, her voice quivering.

Damien remembered the universal remote he'd set up for his mom on the arm of the sofa and grabbed at it, pressing buttons frantically until the lights finally came on.

The second the darkness was devoured by the overhead light, the skeleton fell to pieces. It sounded like someone dropped a xylophone as the bones scattered across the hardwood floor.

The twins were frozen, unable to move, utterly aghast as they looked at one another.

"Damien!" their mother yelled from her bedroom. "You'd better not be making a mess in the kitchen!"

This snapped them out of it. Dorian jumped up and started to shakily gather the bones back into the sheet.

"Sorry, Mom!" Damien called back. "I couldn't sleep. Just getting some cereal!"

"Don't leave the milk out again," she called back, the last of it came out as more of a yawn.

When it was clear she wasn't getting up, Damien knelt and helped his sister gather the bones.

"We have to get rid of them," Dorian said as they stood, her brother holding the sheet like a large sack.

"I'm taking this outside. Wait here," Damien told his sister.

"Where are you going to hide it?" Dorian asked.

"Under the porch?" Damien suggested.

"That'll have to do, I guess," Dorian said.

When he returned, the twins knew they wouldn't be able to get back to sleep that night. They went back upstairs and sat in Damien's room and went over everything that had happened, trying to gain some understanding. They'd turned off the lights, except for the lamp in Damien's room, to ensure their mom wouldn't bother them if she got up any more that night.

"Are we both delulu?" Dorian asked. "Having the same nightmare?"

"It wouldn't be the first time," Damien laughed nervously.

"Remember that dream we both kept having about the clown?"

"I blame the toy chest for that, too." Dorian let out an insincere laugh.

"Did you hear the moaning?" Damien shuttered.

"Yeah," Dorian said softly, "but I don't know if it was a moan, exactly. Almost like a deep, low whistling. Like wind blowing through the rib cage or something."

"Whatever it was, I didn't like it," Damien said.

"Me either," Dorian agreed.

The twins lay awake in silence for a long time. Dorian was on the bed and Damien was sprawled out on the floor, staring up at the ceiling. Both were attempting to make sense of the bag of bones when they began to hear it again, that familiar rattling, but this time farther away and more muffled.

"It can't be!" Damien looked at his sister.

"It happened once," Dorian said weakly, "it was bound to happen again."

Damien stood and listened for the sound, trying to figure out which direction it was coming from.

"Surely it can't get inside!" Damien said. "It doesn't have anything to grip a doorknob!"

"That might not stop it," Dorian said, her eyes wide as she stared at the window of the second story bedroom. "Look."

Damien turned to see a figure at the window, which was still open from earlier in the evening, not even a screen in place to separate them from the ghostly figure. Its windy wailing was louder than before, more like a shriek than a moan, and the sheet draped over it was blowing eerily in the breeze.

"What do you want?" Dorian begged, frightened but curious.

The sheet drifted off the body and flitted away in the wind, landing somewhere on the roof of the porch.

"I don't think it can hurt us," Damien said.

"How do you know?" Dorian asked.

"It couldn't even get the sheet off; the wind blew it off." Damien moved closer to the window, slowly.

Dorian stood back but asked again, "What do you want?"

"Something's wrong, the skull doesn't look right to me," Damien said.

Dorian stared at the two empty eye sockets observing them through the window and realized something was missing. "The jawbone is gone!"

"Mandible," Damien whispered, not looking away from the skeleton to see the scowl he knew he was getting from Dorian.

The thing slowly, gently blew into the bedroom and floated toward the bed and pointed down.

Dorian was unafraid now. She knelt at the edge of the bed and looked under and saw the mandible. She reached out and picked it up, holding it up towards the skeleton. A skeletal hand seemingly held together by nothingness reached out to grasp the missing bone and placed it where it belonged. The very second the skeleton was complete, the wind swept up the bones into a whirlwind that spun into a cyclone. Papers began to blow about the room, and the lamp blew onto the floor and shattered. The twins covered their eyes and crouched down to shield themselves from the growing tornado in Damien's room. The wailing wind was now tempered with tumultuous laughter and the sound of wind chimes made of bone.

Then, as though it had never happened, it stopped. The wind was gone, and with it the bag of bones that had tormented the twins that night.

"What on earth?!" Their mother barged into the room. "I thought you outgrew all that roughhousing! It's late and you two should be in bed!"

In shock, the twins looked at one another knowingly and smiled.

"Sorry, Mom," they said in unison.

* * *

The next day was Halloween, and being in Salem, that meant it would be a half day, which was lucky because the twins were exhausted from the events of the night before. They were also grounded because of the mess their mom had assumed was caused by them, but they didn't put up a fight about coming straight home after school to clean it up and to hand out candy to the neighborhood kids. After retrieving their bikes, the twins walked them toward home. When they got to the edge of Salem Woods, they paused only a second before silently agreeing to leave their bikes and go to try to find the spot where they'd found the bones in the first place. They searched and searched, but knowing they'd be in trouble if they stayed out too late, they eventually gave up looking. Just as they were about to turn and leave, they heard a voice. It sounded like a man reading a story aloud. They followed the sound until they could see a group of people, some in costumes, a few in snarky sweaters from the shops downtown, some in matched bachelorette party t-shirts.

The people were standing around a man dressed in a t-shirt and jeans, which were starkly contrasted by his cape and a top hat. He was carrying a walking stick and a lantern, though it was still light out.

"Tour guides," Dorian huffed.

"Hey, at least he shelled out for a cape and a lantern to set the mood," Damien laughed.

"What are they doing all the way out here, anyway?" Dorian asked.

Her brother shrugged. "Must be new."

Several middle-aged women in tiny witch hats giggled at a less than mediocre joke as the twins started to leave. Before they could get too far, they overheard the tour guide say, "The spirit of a forlorn soldier wanders these woods." The twins stopped in their tracks and turned back to the tour guide as he continued. "Came to meet his lover so they could run away together. Instead, her father caught wind of the plan and set out to stop the meeting by orchestrating a huge snare to trap him. The soldier set foot in this very clearing and was immediately trapped, hanging from the branches of this tree in a burlap sack."

There was muttering among the tourists in the group as the guide paused to take a long drink from his water bottle.

"I think this could be easily debunked since it would be difficult to catch a man of average height and weight in a burlap sack snare trap, but that's the story as it was told to me. As you know, this is the Salem Specter Skeptics Tour."

"What happened to the soldier after that?" a goth teen asked from the group.

"The story goes like this: the father of the young woman had intended to come and release the soldier the next morning, after he'd sent his daughter away to Boston to be with her cousins. As it turns out that night there was a terrible storm, a Nor'easter. Poor guy froze to death out there in that burlap sack before he could be released."

A few gasps escaped the crowd along with more muttering.

"And thus, the soldier walks these woods at night, searching for his lost love."

"Sick!" the goth teen said. The tour group laughed.

"Maybe now that he's got his jawbone back, he'll stick to the woods," Dorian said as they turned to go home.

"Guess he couldn't keep it together without his mandible," Damien deadpanned.

"You have a lucrative career as a tour guide ahead of you," Dorian said.

"Salem: the only place where you can start an entire business with only ghost stories and dad jokes."

Justin felt the fly land on his ear, its tiny legs tickled the skin of his lobe, and he swatted at it. At first the fly took off, but it quickly landed on Justin's other ear, and before he could flick it off, the fly crawled into the darkness of his inner ear. He shook his head side to side, all the while feeling the scratch of the creature's legs inside his ear as it burrowed deeper in.

He heard the deep hum of the fly as it slowly made itself comfortable in the tunnel it had discovered. Justin crammed a finger into the tight space, attempting to force it out, or kill it so it would fall out as he shook his head. He only succeeded in forcing the fly deeper into his ear, and the buzzing suddenly became an echo inside his cavernous head.

When he told his mother about it, she sat him down and shined her flashlight down Justin's ear, but insisted she couldn't see a thing.

"You're probably just imagining it's still in there because you didn't see it fly out. There's no way it could get so far in there we wouldn't be able to see it." His mom patted his head, but Justin still heard the low buzz of the fly making its home within his head.

The next morning, Justin's eyes were blood shot and a little swollen, his head was pounding and he was exhausted, having been kept

awake all night by the incessant humming. When his mother placed breakfast in front of him, she could see that he was unwell and was not surprised when he refused it. She placed a hand on his forehead.

"I don't think you should go to school today," she told him, and he was relieved, knowing he would spend the day on the couch playing video games. Besides, there was no way he could pay attention in class with the buzz, buzz, buzz echoing in his head.

In the early afternoon, Justin realized he hadn't heard the annoying zip within his head and thought maybe he'd just needed to get his mind off the fly. Maybe his mother was right and he'd just scared himself into thinking it hadn't escaped. He realized just how tired he was, and curled up on the couch to finally get some sleep.

He awoke late, well after dark. He immediately felt the pain in his forehead and groaned. He heard a strange sound within his head, like something squishy rolling around against his brain. The idea that the fly might be in there, alive and trying to get out, sickened him. He jolted for the bathroom, where he splashed water at his face and then slapped his cheeks with his palms, trying to get himself to pull it together. Then, all at once, the noise ceased and there was quiet once again. Justin shook his head at himself in the mirror. You're cracking up, he thought to himself, and realized his face was quite pale, his eyes even redder than they had been earlier.

"Justin, is that you?" his mother called from her room. "Are you okay?"

"Yeah, Mom, I just don't feel good," he called back. She got up and took his temperature, but it was normal, so she put him to bed. "If you don't feel better tomorrow, I'll call Doctor Brundle."

The next morning, Justin was awakened by the sound of intense drone within his skull. This time, it seemed to make a ferocious sound, as though an entire beehive had nested there. He felt so ill he couldn't get out of bed that day, and once again his mother kept him home from school. She called the doctor, but he gave her the usual recommendation of "rest and fluids."

By the end of the week, after one visit to the pediatrician and plenty of rest and fluids, Justin's pallor was turning a strange gray color with a dark shadow around his deeply bloodshot eyes. He'd lost weight in his arms and legs, and his cheekbones were well-defined, the headache made him too nauseous to eat. He swore to his mother he heard the fly in his head because it made terrible sounds throughout the day and night. She assured him it was just a terrible headache, like the doctor had said, and tried to feed him a bowl of broth to calm him before leaving him to rest. She said that if he wasn't better by morning, she would take him to the hospital, on the doctor's orders.

In the middle of the night, Justin was once again awakened by the intense pain in his cranium and the sound of buzzing deep within. He sat up on his bed and tried to call out for his mother, but only the sound of the loud hum came out, more amplified by the hollow of his mouth. He attempted to scream for help as he felt something awful welling up within his head and braced himself.

First, he felt the tickle of many legs inside his right ear, and he thought the fly was finally leaving; until he felt the tiny legs against the skin of his other ear. The annoying, tickling, scratching feeling sent Justin into a frenzy as he shook, attempting to relieve both the noise and the pain. He caught site of one fly that had emerged and fluttered away from him, then another, and another, all zooming out from his ears.

As his mouth widened to once again try and call for his mother, the buzzing grew more ferocious and suddenly, a single, very large horse fly managed its way out of his throat. Justin heaved, the sickness bubbling up within him as the hum of what was inside of him grew louder. He once again braced himself and clutched the blankets on his bed as he widened his jaws, releasing a black, buzzing cloud as

hundreds of flies soared out of him. They poured from his lips and came one by one from his nostrils and as they rushed from his ears, he saw the insects begin to cover his bed and walls, the sound of buzzing filling his bedroom with the deep hum of their wings.

CAMP CARPENTER

Tommy Poole arrived late in the night, when most of the cabins at Camp Carpenter were already darkened, the inhabitants tucked snug in their bunks. As he approached the only cabin with illumination coming from inside, he heard someone telling a story in a hushed tone. Tommy peeked in the window to see a group of kids seated around a boy holding a flashlight at his chin, drenching his face with light and filling the cabin with an eerie glow. The campers were all dressed their pajamas, some seated on the bunks, others on pillows or the trunks that held the items they'd packed for the summer. As Tommy looked into the window, he realized he didn't know any of these kids and wondered if they were all new to Camp Carpenter.

The boy with the flashlight's face twisted into a demonic smile as he spoke. "Fifty years ago, on the first night at camp, one of the kids decided to sneak out to go fishing while his bunkmates slept. He took a flashlight and a fishing pole and headed for the dock. He quietly took a canoe out on the lake, paddling softly, hoping not to wake anyone."

Tommy decided not to interrupt the story, and leaned against the side of the cabin, waiting to hear the rest.

"While he was fishing, the camper heard growling from the nearby woods and caught the glint of two eyes in the darkness at shore.

He'd been warned about the bears before and was so startled that he dropped the fishing pole in the water. It belonged to his bunkmate and he hadn't asked to borrow it, so he had to get it back before it drifted away. It was caught in the slight current, and he lunged to grab it before it floated out of reach. That was his first mistake. He leaned too far over and fell into the water."

Tommy smirked; he'd heard enough scary stories to know exactly where this was going. He guessed that the kid would drown and listened for the moment that happened, planning to burst through the doors and scare his new bunk mates. The voice from within continued the story.

"He was a good swimmer, but his foot got caught on weeds in the water and he was trapped. The water was deep, but if he stretched, he could get his head slightly above the water and get air, so he gulped in a breath and went under to try and free his ankle. It took a few tries, but he managed to get loose."

Tommy cupped his ear to listen, realizing he'd heard this one before. The narrator's voice got quieter to build suspense.

"He hadn't realized how far he was from the shore, and the boat had floated away. It was now very dark, and without a flashlight the camper couldn't make out the shape of the boat, so he looked for light from the camp and began to swim."

And then he gets a cramp and drowns, Tommy thought, and he's doomed to forever haunt camp. The story continued from within the cabin, Tommy awaiting his moment to startle his bunk mates.

"He had almost made it to shore when he got a cramp," the boy continued. Tommy smirked, listening. "And there he drowned, a short swim from the dock."

Tommy's excitement grew as he impatiently awaited his moment.

"Every summer, the ghost returns. We can summon him now, if

you all believe he will come."

Tommy laughed, knowing he was really going to get them.

"I need a few of you to place your hands here, the Ouija board will summon him," the voice stated in a low whisper.

"That's baloney!" another kid said, and Tommy smiled. He was about to scare the living crap out of that camper.

"You think so? Put your hands on it and let's see what happens," the narrator said. Then it got quiet, and Tommy listened, silently moving into position.

"We summon you Tommy, the drowned camper," the speaker said loudly. Tommy furled his brow.

"Thomas Poole," the voice said, and once again, Tommy listened intently. "We summon you to this cabin."

There was silence, save the sound of lake water lapping against the shore, birds in the distance, and a chorus of chirping crickets from the grass.

"We summon you, Thomas Poole! We demand your presence!" the narrator spoke authoritatively, and Tommy was pulled into the cabin, as though he no longer had control over his body.

The campers screamed at the sight of him, for Thomas Poole had been dead more than fifty years. His skin was shriveled and tinged with blue and yellow, the bones visible through his pallid arms and legs. The black holes where his eyes once were appeared hollow, nothing but darkness stared back at the cabin full of children, who stared back with gaping mouths, terrified.

Realizing this was his moment, Tommy raised a skeletal hand, pointed at the boy who had narrated his story, and said,

The lobby of Collins Funeral Home was tastefully decorated; an oriental rug stretched out the length of the wide room, which was lined with fake ferns in planters. At one end of the room there was a set of ornate double doors, propped open to reveal a darkened chapel where slants of light came in through the tall, narrow windows. Pews lined either side of an aisle that led straight up to an open casket surrounded by fresh floral arrangements. The realization shook Erik, but only for a moment before he reminded himself that this would be a daily occurrence if he was offered the sales job. He'd called for an interview after seeing a job vacancy ad in the newspaper.

"That's a Chandler Opulence," an older gentleman said from behind Erik. "Top of the line casket. Built to keep everything out, and keep everything else in." He laughed and added a wink so quick most people might have missed it. "I'm Jack Collins," he finished, a bit more serious. Erik stared at him, unsure whether to laugh at the joke or ignore it. He chose the latter.

"Mr. Collins, thanks for meeting with me. I'm Erik Singer, we spoke on the phone. Pleased to meet you," Erik spoke strongly, clearly, and

with a smile. He reached out to shake hands with Mr. Collins, who grunted and began to walk toward the open chapel doors. Erik was slightly offended, but he followed the large, white-haired man.

Mr. Collins stood in the doorway, inspecting the setup of the darkened chapel. Erik glanced down the length of the aisle. He normally would've looked away at the sight of a dead body, but he instead chose to look closely at the casket itself while trying not to let his eyes fall directly onto the person inside. He knew he'd have to be comfortable with it if he was going to work there, but he hadn't got the job yet. Erik squinted at the casket, which was placed in between two slants of light, leaving it in light shadow that only allowed him to make out some of the detail. The casket was gray or silver, with a white lining. The handles were sculpted, but it was too dim for Erik to make out much detail beyond that.

"Chandler Opulence, you say? Couldn't choose a better option myself," Erik said. He knew little about the product but wanted to impress the man who might soon be his boss. Mr. Collins nodded his agreement. Erik continued, "I'd like to get a closer look—important to know the product."

"You can't sell what you don't know... inside and out," Mr. Collins laughed. "Your resume said you have sales experience?"

"Yessir. Two years in telesales and one in automotive," Erik said confidently. "If you can sell a car, you can sell anything."

"Selling a casket is a lot like selling a car. People want comfort and style, but it ultimately comes down to the budget," Mr. Collins said.

"... and how much wiggle room there is in that budget," Erik asserted. Mr. Collins smirked.

"Fine line between helping a mourning widow and taking her for a ride, son. Be sure you remember that when you take your first consult," Mr. Collins said with a smile.

"The customer always comes first," Erik said. He was having difficulty hiding his excitement as he realized he may have just landed the job.

"Save the corporate talk, kid. I've got a busy afternoon: viewing, services, and burial, all in a day's work." Mr. Collins pulled a pocket watch from his suit to check the time. "Mourners will be arriving for the wake any moment."

"Thank you for the opportunity," Erik stuck his hand out to Mr. Collins, but he'd already begun walking the length of the hallway toward his office. Erik shrugged, he'd heard Mr. Collins was tough as nails.

Erik stepped outside, where he nearly ran into Cindy Collins, the co-owner of the facility.

"I'm sorry, I didn't see you coming," Erik said politely.

"Oh goodness, you're Erik Singer, aren't you? I forgot to call and cancel the interview." She seemed scattered.

"I had a great talk with Mr. Collins. I'm really looking forward to working with you," Erik said, reaching his hand out, hoping someone would shake it.

"I beg your pardon?" Cindy asked, surprised and dismayed.

"We just spoke. Mr. Collins met me in the lobby—"

"Mr. Collins, my father, is dead," Cindy said, removing her dark sunglasses to reveal red, swollen eyes.

"That can't be, I just saw him—"

"Laid out in the chapel for viewing? What kind of a sick joke is this, anyway?" Cindy asked, pushing past Erik. "I need to finish setting up for the wake."

He followed Cindy into the lobby, confused. She strode to the chapel entryway, where she threw the lights on.

There, in the Chandler Opulence, was the man Erik had just spoken with.

THE PIER

Aimee watched Evan gallop down the wooden pier of The Willows. It was a cold day for June, and persistent fog and drizzle had discouraged other visitors to the park on Salem Sound. The ocean was grey and choppy, rolling up over the rocky shoreline with increasing force. Aimee started to scold Evan for running, but she stopped herself. He had been so disappointed that the ice cream stand was closed, and she didn't want to spoil more of the little boy's fun. Evan made horse hoof clopping sounds as he bounded, and she heard him shout, "Woah, Nelly!" when he approached the railing at the end of the pier.

"Howdy, Lone Ranger!" Aimee greeted him as she met him at the rail.

"I'm not a Lone Ranger. I'm just a cowboy," he replied.

"Oh, I'm sorry. Pleased to meet you, Justin Cowboy."

"Nooo... Just a—"

Suddenly a large wave crested and crashed through the railing. Aimee grabbed Evan's hand as the water drenched them. As the wave retreated, she looked at Evan, waiting for him to start bawling. Instead, he started to giggle.

"Surprise! The ocean gotcha!"

Aimee laughed along. "Hey, it got you, too! Come on, it's too cold to stay out and play now that we're wet. We have to get going."

Evan took Aimee's hand, and they began to walk back down the pier. Aimee's shoes squished with every step. Evan stopped and looked down at his feet.

"Yeah, my shoes are wet too, buddy. Let's get you home to dry off."

Evan stood still, staring down. Aimee realized he wasn't looking at his feet, but at the gap between the deck boards beneath them. She could see the dark water and foamy white caps of the waves moving back and forth below.

"Come on, Evan. We have to go. Your mom will be home soon."

"I don't like the ocean surprises," Evan whispered, more to the deck boards than to Aimee. "They're scary."

"You were laughing at it a minute ago. It's not going to hurt you. The waves are getting big because there is a storm far out in the sea."

Evan glanced up at Aimee, his eyes wide, their joyful blue now a tempestuous gray, and exclaimed in a grave tone, "Sometimes the ocean hurts people, like sailors. Sea monsters eat them!"

"There's no such thing as sea monsters, buddy, but we do have to get moving. The waves are getting too big."

Aimee coaxed the little boy along the pier. He stepped carefully, one board at a time, eyeing the ocean suspiciously through the gaps. The wind began whipping at their backs, and the water frothed angrily through the pier boards. Evan came to a hard stop. He again gazed at his feet and whispered something, but the wind stole his voice away from Aimee's ears.

"We gotta go," she urged Evan loudly, trying to push him along from behind. The little boy began to wail, frozen on the spot, and Aimee had to pick him up around the waist and lope awkwardly toward the shore.

His cries morphed from a primal howl into an intelligible word: "Monster!"

"There's no monsters, buddy."

His screams ebbed into a whimper. "Monster, monster."

As Aimee stepped off the wooden pier and onto the dirt path of the seaside park, she put him down on solid ground. Crouching down to look him in the eye, Aimee reassured him again, "No monsters, I promise." They heard another huge wave crash against the rail, and they both turned to watch it.

"Surprise!" Aimee said to Evan, smiling and trying to buoy the boy's mood with a jovial tone. "The ocean didn't get us that time!"

Then she noticed something strange appear between the balusters of the rail near the far end of the pier. Squinting to see through the fog and mist, she thought she saw something slide through the gaps, reaching and grabbing at the deck boards. It looked like a pair of tentacles, dark, muscular, and bigger than her arm. Aimee looked down at the little boy, and saw him staring at it, too.

"Surprise..." he replied weakly, clutching her hand.

YOU CAN HAVE IT

Gregory was only five when his parents decided it was time to move into a bigger home. They often spent their summer weekends driving to open houses throughout the neighborhoods his parents were interested in. They'd already been to three other houses and as they pulled up to a ranch style home on a cul-de-sac, his mother looked at his father in dismay.

"Oh no, I can't believe it!" Greg's mom looked horrified when she saw the house.

"What's wrong, Sharon?" Greg's dad asked, looking over at his wife as he put the car in park.

She was about to speak, but glanced to the back seat, remembering Greg was in the car with them.

"Never mind," his mom said. "Let's get through this one fast. I'm starving, Brian."

"I know it doesn't look like much from the outside, but it has a pool," Greg's dad said as they got out of the car. "And it's priced to sell. In this market, we'd be lucky—"

"I don't like the neighborhood," Greg's mom said. Greg rolled his eyes, following behind his parents. She hated every house they'd looked at that day. "And anyway," she continued,

"it's probably priced to sell for a reason."

She was so uninterested that Greg's mom rushed through the viewing, barely stopping at each room to look, having already made up her mind this house wasn't the one. Greg had tired of the whole process, and so when the owner of the house suggested viewing the garage, Greg quietly turned the other direction and crept down a long hallway that was lined with empty spaces where portraits and art used to hang. He could see the outline of where the frames had been, and a few nails still stuck out of the paneling. The house had already mostly been packed up, and there were boxes stacked in most of the rooms. All of the furniture had been taken apart or wrapped in moving blankets or padding, ready to be taken away. Greg had stopped in the master bedroom and stood on his tippy toes to look out of the windows that overlooked the pool in the backyard. He sighed, knowing his parents didn't like the size of the house, so the likelihood of ever getting to swim in that pool was pretty low.

He heard a sound coming from a room across the hall and recognized it as a child making car noises. Following the quiet "vroom-vroom" sounds he discovered a small boy, about his own age, playing with toy cars in a closet.

"Want to play with me?" the boy asked as he pushed the little toy car along the railing at the bottom of the sliding closet doorway.

"Sure!" Greg replied and took the car that was offered to him.

"What's your name?" the boy asked.

"Gregory," he said, "but you can call me Greg."

"I'm Billy," the boy said.

"Why are you moving?" Greg asked.

"My mom's been really sad," Billy told him. "She doesn't like it here anymore."

"Yeah," Greg replied. "My mom's having another baby and she's sad our house is too small. I don't want a little sister, though."

"I wish I had a brother or sister," Billy said. "I think maybe my mom wouldn't be so sad."

Greg thought over this for a moment and slowly nodded, wondering if his mom would be happier with a bigger family. He hoped she would.

He realized then that he felt cold, although it was a sweltering August afternoon.

Seeing him shiver, Billy asked, "Are you cold?"

"A little," Greg said, and then pointed at a nearby floor vent.

"Gregory!" He heard his mother calling for him from down the hallway. He stood up, still holding the little car.

"Here," Greg said as he held out the toy to Billy.

"I don't need it anymore; you can have it," the boy said, and Greg got up and left the little ranch home with his parents.

"Hurry up," his father said. "Your mother is already in the car." He noticed the toy in Greg's hand. "Where did that come from?"

"The kid in the house gave it to me," Greg said.

"What kid?" his father asked.

"The boy in the closet," Greg said. His father stopped and turned toward his son.

"This wasn't an open house," his dad said. "We were the only family viewing it today."

"He lives here," Greg insisted, then paused. "Or used to… I guess."

"We saw every room in that house," his father asserted. "There was no little boy."

"But I saw him—"

"You have to stop making up stories, Gregory," his father said. "You have a very big imagination, but it's important to be honest. Tell me the truth. If you took that toy, we need to give it back."

"I didn't take it, though," Greg insisted.

"Stealing is wrong, Gregory," his father spoke sternly. "I thought you'd learned this lesson with that pack of gum at the store."

"But I—" Greg began to sniffle.

"Come along, son," his father said, turning the boy back toward the house. "We're going to give it back and apologize for snooping around."

His father marched him up to the front door and rang the bell.

Greg looked up at his father's profile and could see the frustration on his face. He knew stealing was wrong, and that's why Greg would never have taken something that didn't belong to him. When he took the pack of gum he didn't know better, but now he did. He'd learned his lesson.

The woman who had shown them around the house appeared in the doorway, and through tears, Greg said, "I'm sorry. I took this." He held up the toy car for the woman to see.

"Where did you find this?" the woman asked. "We thought we'd packed up all of the toys…"

He wiped away a tear and told her, "The kid in the house."

"What kid?" his father asked, frustrated.

"Billy," Greg said. "He told me I could have it because he didn't need it anymore."

The woman in the doorway pressed a hand over her lips and stared down in shock at the toy Greg held up for her to take.

"I'm very sorry, ma'am," Greg's father said, handing the toy to the woman, who reluctantly took it. He then pulled Greg

away by his hand, practically dragging him to the car.

"What was all that about?" Greg's mother asked once they were in the vehicle.

"Greg found a toy in that house and took it. Tried to blame it on some kid he made up named Billy. That was a lie, so I made him take it back and apologize. That toy belongs to someone else," his father replied.

"Oh dear," his mother said. "I should've said something, but it was so horrible, I didn't want to say it in front of Greg, but now…"

"Now what?" His father urged.

"Well," she said, "a little boy named Billy used to live in that house."

"See!" Greg yelled from the back seat. "I told you so!"

"The thing is…" his mother's face was pale. "Oh goodness, that poor woman." She stopped, hesitant to continue.

"Just say it, Sharon," his father pressed her to continue.

"A few years ago, you remember that story in the news about the little boy they found in the closet—"

"My god, that was this house? Why didn't you say something?"

Sharon gestured to Greg, who was buckled in and listening intently.

"It's ok, Mom," Greg said. "I knew he was a ghost. I didn't think dad would believe me if I told him that part."

THE ABOMINABLE GRUMBALD

Leaves scraped along the sidewalk,
The wind their puppeteer.
They danced along, and glided,
Over there and over here.

The children grabbed their buckets,
Plastic pumpkins, witches, and ghosts,
To carry all through town,
And see who got the most.
Demons, monsters, and ghouls,
Ran rampant in the street,
From house to house and door to door
To gather up their treats!

A chill was in the air that year,
And how the wind did blow!
As the evening sky grew dark,
There came an early snow.
The first snow on Halloween,
In a several years or more,
But still the children carried on,
Dashing from door to door.

No one could have guessed,
That the Grumbalo would appear,
That on this Halloween,
There was something more to fear.
The wind began to howl,
The leaves blew by and by,
Mothers held their children close,
"It's the Grumbalo!" someone cried.

The people scattered, screaming,
Searching for places to hide,
Fathers grabbed tiny hands
And dragged their children inside.
Doors were slammed and locked,
The streets went silent, then,
Except for the fallen leaves,
That were dragged along by the wind.

Candy and masks lay all about,
As snow dusted the ground,
And when the wind halted,
There came a horrible sound.
Like a growl and a groan in the distance,
The kind you feel in your bones,
This was the sound of hunger,
The call of the Grumbalo.

With a gallop he appeared,
The trees shook as he passed,
And when his feet found pavement,
There he stopped, at last.
The creature sniffed the air,
For the thing he craved;
Warm-blooded children,
To carry off to his cave.

The Grumbalo was starving,
He had not hunted in years,
And the grumble in his gut,
Came with a thirst for fear.
Dirty, patchy fur from head to foot,
With claws of solid black,
His eyes were huge and green,
His spine showed through his back.

The Grumbalo was gigantic,
Twelve feet tall, at least,
But the most terrifying thing,
Were the large and gnarled teeth.
His body seemed thin and waning,
The ribs showed through his sides,
And as the monster panted,
His breath came out in white.

The Grumbalo leaned forward,
Sniffing the air again,
And he caught the scent of a child,
One who didn't make it in.
He lurched toward the smell,
The ground rumbled beneath his feet,
He shook the bushes until,
A child crawled out from underneath.

It was a little boy named Johnny,
And he stood up tall and brave,
He faced the monster alone,
"Go on! Take me to your cave!"
Johnny shook hard in his devil costume,
The mask still on his face,
He stared hard into the Grumbalo's eyes,
And waited to be taken away.

The Grumbalo sucked in a breath,
And released it in a growl,
That blew off Johnny's mask,
And whipped back his red cowl.
Johnny clenched his fists,
And drew all the air he could hold,
Then released it in a screech
That surprised the Grumbalo.

The monster sniffed at Johnny,
Smelling his head and his face,
And then to Johnny's shock,
The Grumbalo stepped away.
The creature slumped down on the grass,
Like a dog awaiting a treat.
Johnny pulled out a handful of candy,
And held it out to the beast.

The Grumbalo let out a grunt,
And swiped at Johnny's hand,
Knocking the candy to the ground,
Johnny didn't understand.
The monster was terribly hungry,
And a handful wasn't enough,
He reached out for Johnny's bucket,
And Johnny looked down at his stuff.

The bucket was filled to the top,
With many sweet delights,
But he could see the beast was starving,
So he did what he thought was right.
He held out the bucket before him,
The Grumbalo took his prize,
And placing the handle between his teeth,
He scooped up Johnny's disguise.

A giant claw pulled at the cowl,
And replaced the devil mask,
The Grumbalo straightened up,
But Johnny just had to ask,
"You mean you don't want to eat me?"
The Grumbalo turned from the child,
And without so much as a grunt,
He galloped back into the wild.

Johnny's parents held him tight,
He thought he'd never get free.
When they asked how he knew what to do,
Johnny said laughingly,
"The Grumbalo was starving,
He only wanted a treat,
And no one should go without candy,
Especially on Halloween!

So if it snows on Halloween,
While you trick or treat,
Be sure to ask for extra,
For the Grumbalo to eat!

APPARITIONS

The first time Amelia saw the ghost she ran straight for her parent's bedroom, where she refused to leave until the sun was up the following morning. He'd appeared in the middle of the night at the foot of her bed, wringing his hands and wailing, **"GET OUT!"** over and over in agony. She'd done exactly as he said and threw her blankets to the floor and got out of there.

The following morning, she pleaded with her dads to move out of their new home—a historic structure in a small town, which they'd moved into only a week before. It was a beautiful, old Victorian mansion with a sweeping history that had included everything from housing a famous stage actor to a fire in the 1920s. The house had been restored and added onto over the years, but it still had many of the original details, including several old pieces of furniture and a few antique Tiffany lamps. Amelia had loved the history and was excited to live in a house with such interesting stories to tell, but that was before she'd known there would be ghosts.

"Daddy, he doesn't want us here. He'll be angry if we don't leave, and then who knows what he'll do?" Amelia had tried to reason, but her dads just wouldn't listen.

"Oh sweetheart, you must have had a nightmare," one dad said. "That's all, just your imagination. You don't believe in ghosts, do you?"

Amelia frowned up at him.

"And anyway, we can't move now, we just got here!" the other added.

Her two fathers tried to make her see the logic.

"It's just nerves; we moved to a new town and you're starting at a new school this week. That's a lot of stress, and sometimes stress gives you nightmares. Remember how nervous you were about that swim meet last year? You had nightmares for a week." Her dad wrapped a blanket around her shoulders and gave her a squeeze.

"Maybe you're right," she relaxed a little, comforted by this notion. Still, she tossed and turned for the rest of the night, even after her parents stayed up a while with her. After a few nights of quiet, she began to accept her dad's explanation.

The next time it appeared, the apparition loomed over Amelia's bed, translucent and glowing. She sank into the mattress and pulled the covers up and over her head, but she could still hear his awful cries.

"GET OUT! GET OUT OF THIS HOUSE!" he screamed with an urgency that hadn't been present before. When she gathered the courage to throw back the sheets so she could run to her dad's room, she saw his face and froze in fright as he screeched at her, **"GO! GO NOW!"** His eyes were pale white, his mouth opening wide for him to shriek his command at her. When she managed to unfreeze, she took off down the hall to her parent's room, where she collapsed in a fit of tears at the foot of their bed.

When her father had calmed her enough, he accompanied her down the hall and to her bedroom, where he tucked her in and checked the room for the ghost.

"See, sweetheart? No ghosts, not even under the bed or in the closet," he said.

"That's because he only appears out of thin air, Papa," Amelia whimpered.

"Would it help if I stayed with you a while?" Papa asked. She nodded. He sat with her until she fell asleep and turned off the light as he left her room.

Amelia was once again awakened by the shrieking ghost, circling above her bed. The girl sat bolt upright, frightened, but looking on as the wraith angrily whirled in the space above her bed, as though he were pacing the room.

"GET OUT! GET OUT OR YOU'LL ALL BE DEAD!" he warned and flew to face the child on the bed. If he'd been a solid being, his nose would've been against her own. She felt the cold of his scream against her skin as her hair blew back.

"GET OUT NOW!" he screeched.

This terrified her so greatly that Amelia darted for the door and down the stairs, where she was greeted with a wall of flames that had engulfed the kitchen and living room. She bolted back up the stairs and woke her dads, who quickly devised a plan of escape out the window. By the time they were all on the ground below, a fire truck was arriving.

"What a tragedy! When the realtor mentioned there had been a fire here a hundred years ago, I never expected it would happen again!" Papa said. "I'm just glad we all made it out safely."

"Imagine if Amelia hadn't woken us up!" Daddy said, looking

down at his daughter.

Amelia looked up at the flame-swallowed house and the realization swept over her what the ghost had been trying to convey. The spirit that had scared her had only been trying to warn her of the danger. Then, she saw the face of her guardian in the window of her bedroom. She detected a smile, and returned it, no longer afraid.

"Amelia, baby, what are you smiling at?" Papa asked, holding her close.

"My friend."

THE EGUH

It came from the mountain,

The Eguh Rets Nom,

Ate all the children,

Then swallowed their moms.

He loved the taste of children,

So yummy and so sweet,

But spit out all the mothers,

Because they taste like feet.

A PORTRAIT OF BETSY

Little Jeff O'Malley was different. That's what everyone said.

He stared too long at people, stood far away from the kids playing at recess, and ate the same lunch every single day. Jeff didn't speak up often, but when he did, the other kids would wish they hadn't interacted with him in the first place. The teachers drew straws at the beginning of each year to see who'd have Jeff in their class. So, when Mrs. Ward drew the short straw her coworkers expected dismay, but she was no stranger to being labeled as odd herself. She looked forward to challenging the other teachers' views of Jeff O'Malley the way she had challenged their views of her. She'd recognized all the signs of being "different" in this particular pupil. No teacher had ever put in the effort with Jeff and Jeff knew this year would be different when Mrs. Ward had taken a special interest in him. He didn't like anybody, but if he ever came close to liking another person, Mrs. Ward was as close as he could get.

So, when Mrs. Ward had asked Jeff to draw a picture of Betsy, Jeff did exactly what he was told.

It was early in the school year, when September was still warm with long, sunny days. The teacher knew the heat would have her class distracted and testy, so instead of another math lesson, she opted for partnered portrait drawing. She placed a basket of crayons on each of

the tables. The children's hands went for them, like wolf cubs fighting over their mother's fresh kill. Jeff waited patiently for his tablemates to finish finding their crayons, and when they had dispersed, he went digging in the dirty rainbow of broken wax. He first pulled out a tiny bright red crayon, then the back half of a brown one with no label, and lastly a black crayon that appeared untouched.

Jeff stared blankly down at the paper in front of him for a moment before looking around the table at the pictures being scribbled away by the other children. Shamika had drawn a huge, pink blob with a face that housed a yellow blob meant to be her partner's blonde curls. Brad drew a stick figure with a baseball cap meant to be Derek. Derek was intent on his drawing of a blue and red mixture that appeared to be a flying... Superman? Jeff stared at the drawing with disdain when he saw that one of his table mates had not followed the directions. When his eyes went to his own paper, it was just an empty page. He slowly looked up and found the eyes of his partner looking at him and then back down at her drawing, which was surprisingly good.

"What's the matter, Jeff?" Mrs. Ward asked, noticing the busy crayons in the other children's hands.

"It's too loud," Jeff said, not moving his eyes from the paper. The teacher paused.

"It's too loud, so you can't draw?" Mrs. Ward asked, hoping to understand him better.

"Yes," he said matter-of-factly, offering no further explanation.

She looked over to Betsy, who he'd been paired up with for this art project. She was drawing away, humming and swaying as she went about her work. She'd never been good at sitting still, but at least she was staying in her seat today.

"Why don't you and Betsy move to the back of the class near the big window?" she urged.

"Ugh," Betsy huffed. "Come on then, let's get this over with." She stood and stomped the length of the classroom, not waiting for Jeff. He slowly sauntered back to where she had taken a seat. Mrs. Ward sighed and made her way up to her desk where she read over the homework she'd be assigning at the end of the day.

At the back of the class there was a giant vintage desk with chairs on either side. Betsy sat facing the classroom, and Jeff took the seat opposite her, facing the big, open windows. The two children observed one another from across the long desk and Betsy's mouth warped into a snarl of discomfort. Jeff watched her, expressionless. She fidgeted a lot, which seemed to make it difficult for Jeff to start his drawing.

"Of course I got stuck with the most boring partner," Betsy said as she put crayon to paper again, muttering to herself and drawing in big, exaggerated movements. Jeff didn't respond, but finally went to work on his drawing, expressionless and silent. He found little enjoyment in artistic projects, but he was skilled at capturing a realistic likeness, the way one draws a diagram or instructions rather than sketching for fun.

When a half hour had passed, ample time for the second graders to finish their portraits, the old kitchen timer on Mrs. Ward's desk rang out, silencing the children. They had been chattering loudly while they worked, some were getting rowdy, having finished their drawings early.

"Children, please bring your portraits to me," Mrs. Ward said. They fell into an unorganized line where they placed their masterpieces face up in a pile before the teacher.

"A wonderful job, Shamika! Good work, Kevin. Very... imaginative, Derek," Mrs. Ward said as each of the students placed their papers before her. When the children were all back in their seats, she saw Jeff sitting alone with his chair turned away, facing the

window. His hands were folded neatly in his lap, and he sat up straight, as he always did.

"Jeff, I didn't see your drawing," the teacher said expectantly. Jeff sat silently, staring ahead, as though he was somewhere far away in his mind.

"Jeff, I asked everyone to bring their drawings to the front, did you not hear?" she asked patiently, the other children snickering and whispering to one another.

Snapping out of his daydreaming, Jeff quietly stood and walked up to the desk and, in contrast with the other children, placed his drawing face down on the desk.

"Where is Betsy?" Mrs. Ward asked without turning the paper over, respecting that Jeff might not have wanted to see her reaction to his art. She would look at it later, in case he was embarrassed about his work on the assignment.

Jeff did not answer.

Mrs. Ward stood, and her eyes searched the room for Betsy. She began to make her way toward the back, sensing something wasn't right. As she approached, she saw a widening lake of brown on the floor from the other side of the desk. Mrs. Ward darted around the vintage desk to find Betsy sprawled on the floor, her mouth and eyes wide open, vomit rolling down her bluish cheek and neck. Her lips and eyes were swollen, and the brown vomit had suddenly turned to a stark white foam.

Realizing Betsy was having an allergic reaction, she asked someone to bring her Betsy's backpack, which she promptly dumped out to search for the EpiPen she knew Betsy carried for her bee allergy. One of the other children had run down the hall and brought back another teacher who had the presence of mind to call 911.

Throughout the chaos, Jeff stood still and watched it all unfold, unfazed by what had happened. Even as the other teacher cleared the room of the other children, Jeff waited silently, forgotten.

Afterward, the paramedics told Mrs. Ward she had saved Betsy's life as they took her out on a stretcher, awake and aware, recovering from her reaction. As the emergency team rolled the gurney by Jeff, Betsy scowled at him, still puffy in the face with the remnants of vomit on the front of her pretty pink dress.

"He did this!" Betsy screamed. "He did something to that bee! He knows I'm allergic!"

The paramedics tried to calm her as they took her from the room, but she carried on about Jeff and the bee all the way out.

Mrs. Ward turned to face Jeff, seeing him nearly unaware, as though he might be in shock.

"Jeff?" Mrs. Ward asked, grabbing his shoulders and leaning down to meet him at eye level. He finally roused and met her gaze.

"Jeff," Mrs. Ward said softly, "Are you alright?"

He looked down at his toes.

"Tell me what happened," she urged.

He remained silent.

"Did you know there was a bee?"

Jeff lifted his gaze, but this time there was an unsettling smile stretched across his face, a blackness in his eyes she had not noticed before.

Mrs. Ward dropped her hands and stood up straight, disturbed.

"Why didn't you tell me about the bee?" Mrs. Ward asked shakily.

"She was finally sitting still enough for me to draw her."

It was then that Mrs. Ward finally turned over the drawing to see a sickeningly detailed portrait of Betsy lying in a pool of brown vomit.

MEG LOOKED UP

Meg toyed with the knob on her locker until she got to the last number in her combination. Did it open? Nope, never on the first try.

Luckily, no one was there to witness her battle with the locker because she was only there to grab her algebra homework after the school had emptied of students. She wouldn't have even made it in if Freddie, the ancient janitor, hadn't been outside for a smoke break. She'd had to bribe him to let her in so late after hours with the last of her tips from her barista job, but at least she wouldn't be late on another of Mr. Wiseman's assignments. He'd already let it slide too many times this semester.

"Open already!" Meg shouted.

She would've asked Freddie to help her with the locker, but after letting her in he'd wandered off, muttering something about dinner like he was a zombie shambling toward fresh brains. The man was a creature of habit, this she knew because he always took his smoke break around 8:00pm, when she was getting out of play rehearsals on Tuesdays. Today was Wednesday and there was no play rehearsal, but she took a chance, hoping she'd catch him outside. She did.

"Come on!" she shouted at the locker. "Open up, you stupid, garbage thing!" She slammed a fist onto the red metal door. It finally popped open.

"Thank you!" she said pushing her glasses back up the bridge of her nose, then looked around, as though she was hoping no one had heard it, regardless of the fact that the only life in the entire building were her, the janitor, and the rats that hid during the daytime. There was no one sharing that hallway with her.

Meg groaned as she realized her algebra book was precariously balanced within the mess of her locker, under everything from old water bottles, graded homework she never took home, tennis shoes she kept there to change into if it rained on her walk to school. She shoved arm up at a right angle to hold everything in place while she tried to perform the surgical removal of her algebra book from the very bottom—a juggling act you only master when you are forced to keep your stuff in a locker. Once the book was out, she knew everything else was in danger of toppling out, so she slammed the red metal door. It clanged closed and then popped back open, whacking her in the nose and breaking her glasses. Everything inside exploded out of the locker. She just stood there and let it happen, realizing she couldn't have stopped it if she tried, and watched as the last piece of paper drifted to the floor like the last leaf letting go of an oak tree branch in early winter.

She sighed, then began to feel something bing warm roll over her lips and down her chin.

"No," Meg said frantically. "No, no, no, no, no!"

Meg cradled her bleeding nose with her left hand and headed for the restroom, leaving the disaster from her locker until she'd taken care of her nose. She felt her heart beating hard as

she pulled her hand away and saw the thick, red liquid. Meg had always hated the sight of blood, and now it was all over her hands and dripping down her white t-shirt. Her anxiety started bubbling up, and it was hard for her to catch her breath. The room spun around her as she tried to ground herself before it turned into a full-on panic attack. The high school's guidance counselor had given her some tricks to try when she felt like this: breathing, counting, and other grounding exercises.

She counted to ten. Then counted backwards down to one. Started over and did it again.

Meg felt her heart rate coming down until she was able to breathe normally again. Although her nerves were shot, she was able to clean herself up and make sure her nose wasn't broken. It wasn't.

She looked in the mirror and tried not to focus on the streaks of blood down the front of her shirt. At least without her glasses it was more of a red blur. Her nose had stopped bleeding, and although her fear of blood had put her on edge, she had to clean up the mess she'd left in the hallway.

When she started for the door, she looked down and realized there was a Hansel and Gretal trail of large, red droplets.

"Freddie's going to kill me," she muttered as she got to the door, but before she could open it, she heard a strange squeaking sound in the hallway. At first she held back, but she decided it was probably Freddie's shoes on the freshly waxed floor and that she'd have to apologize for the mess and explain what happened. When she opened the door, there was no one in the hallway.

"Ew," she said coming out. "Has to be the rats." Then after a pause, "I have to stop talking to myself when I'm nervous."

YOU CAN TALK TO ME, she heard a voice in her head, not unlike her own, but not entirely her own inner monologue.

"Ok, stop being weird," Meg said to herself as she knelt to pick up her things from the floor. She realized just how much blood there was—it was an unusual amount considering how much had been absorbed by her t-shirt. Her stomach churned knowing she'd have to clean it up so she wouldn't get in trouble with Freddie.

As she collected lip gloss, then two pencils, followed by a protractor, she heard a scuffling noise. She looked up from her crouched position, the protractor still in her hand, and saw no one. Deciding her anxiety was just messing with her, she went back to gathering her stuff. She crammed it all back into the locker, a little more organized than it had been before the explosion, and she was able to close the door without much resistance. She let out a sigh of relief and turned to go, algebra book in hand.

I'M STARVING, she heard the voice again in her head and then, I'M SO HUNGRY, MEG.

"Stop it," Meg said aloud, trying to quiet the anxiety building inside her.

It was then that she noticed the footprints, like someone had walked through the droplets of blood on the floor from her nosebleed. Her heart started beating hard again. She was going to clean up the mess so Freddie wouldn't have to, but now she just wanted to get out of there. She started at a fast pace toward the exit, but she was midway down the hall, and it was a long walk to get there.

WHERE ARE YOU GOING, MEG? I'M SO HUNGRY.

She stopped and counted to ten.

Before she could start counting backward, she heard a clanging sound, like someone running across the lockers.

She closed her eyes, afraid to open them, afraid to turn around and see. She was frozen in place as the sound became grotesque, like something being ferociously devoured. Then it got quiet again.

I'M STILL HUNGRY, MEG.

Finally, she opened her eyes and looked all around her, but someone had turned the lights off. She sucked in a breath as fear crept over her. Now, it was dark, but she saw no one at either end of the hallway as her eyes adjusted.

This time she ran. She abandoned her algebra book and made for the exit. There was a scuffling sound behind her, like someone—something—was chasing her. She was too frightened to turn and look. When she got to the door, she pushed as hard as she could, but it wouldn't budge.

Everything stopped. All was quiet again.

Meg counted to ten. She counted backward from ten. She did it again and again until she willed herself to turn around and make a run for the other end of the hallway. She couldn't see much, but she took a deep breath and started off, cautiously jogging in the darkness. It felt like it took forever to get back to the part of the hallway with her locker. As she got closer, she realized there was much more blood than there had been, and that there was something else that wasn't there before. The familiar anxiety filled her chest as terror continued to build within her.

There was Freddie's hat, sitting like an island in a lake of blood.

"Oh my god," Meg whispered, and just as she was about to break into a run again, she felt something warm and wet drip onto her from above.

SOOOOO HUNGRYYYYY.

Meg looked up.

THE BASEMENT

"Why don't you help me down in the basement today?"

Jimmy looked at his father, wide-eyed. He had never been in the basement before. His parents had always said he was too young. Now that he had turned ten, was it possible he was old enough?

"Umm...sure?" Jimmy responded, hesitating in his disbelief.

"Alright, great," responded his father. "If I'm going to get the kitchen redone on time I'm going to need a lot of help."

The house that Jimmy and his parents lived in was an old Victorian. His parents were planning on selling it soon, so they were doing work on the house to modernize it. Jimmy liked the old house and would miss it when they left. He had been there his whole life, and now that he was going to be allowed into the basement, a whole new world had been opened to him.

After breakfast, Jimmy's father led him to the old, dark, grainy wooden basement door. His father slid the slide bolt lock and turned the handle. Jimmy had always watched his father descend, imagining what could be awaiting him. His friend down the street had a T.V. room in his basement, but Jimmy doubted his father had a T.V. down there. Jimmy pictured their basement more like a small cave where his father's treasures were hidden, with crystals glinting in the walls

like the dwarves' mine in Snow White. As his father reached in and pulled the chain to turn on the light in the stairwell, he stepped aside and motioned for Jimmy to head on down.

"Hold the railing, Jimmy."

The stairs were steep and uneven, and the boards squeaked with each step. Tentatively, Jimmy stepped down into the basement, placing one, then two feet on each step before attempting the next, with his father right behind him. When they got to the last step, his father walked past him into the gloom, and then he heard another pull of a chain, and a light came on further into the basement. Looking around, Jimmy saw that it was bigger than he had imagined, and noticeably lacking anything that sparkled like treasure. They were in a large room full of building supplies that his father was using to remodel the kitchen. The naked lightbulbs created deep shadows on the stacks of boards and tile.

"Okay, what I need from you is to hold this flashlight while I work on the pipes for the kitchen. The light here doesn't reach into the little nook where they are." His father pointed behind Jimmy to an area under the stairs. There was a pile of paint cans in front of a small doorway.

"It will be a tight fit, but it shouldn't take us long," his father said as he handed him a flashlight. His father got on his knees and crawled into the entrance way, and Jimmy followed behind. "This would be the time you turn the flashlight on. We can't work in the dark, can we?" his father joked.

Turning on the flashlight, Jimmy gave a quiet yelp as he came face to face with a nest of daddy long-legs. Not wanting to seem scared in front of his father, he covered it up with a cough. He didn't want his father to think he was still too young to be down here.

"Now just shine the light over here while I replace these." His father directed him to an array of pipes along the narrow wall.

While his father worked, Jimmy looked around the little room under the stairs. It was mostly made up of old, bare wood, and stone. He noticed a dark spot on the wall. Looking closer, he noticed the spot looked like the upper half of a person: a distinctive shape of head and shoulders. It looked like the spot was caused by a fire as it seemed to be flakey, like a log that was sitting in a campfire pit. Jimmy reached out and rubbed a finger on the spot, and a piece flaked off.

"Hey, Dad, was there ever a fire in this house?"

Grunting while tightening a pipe, his father replied, "Not that I know of. Keep that light over here."

Looking away from the shape, Jimmy made sure to keep the light focused on his father's work. After a few minutes, his eyes slid back to that dark area with the soot. He couldn't get it out of his head. It looked so much like a person. Twenty minutes later, Jimmy and his father were back in the kitchen, and his dad turned on the faucet.

"Works great. Thanks for the help, Jimmy. Your mother and I wouldn't have been able to fit in that little spot together. Now go on and help your mother upstairs."

Jimmy held his head high, proud he had proved helpful, but he kept thinking about that shape in the basement.

That night as he lay in bed, staring at the ceiling and wondering what could have made it, he heard something from the old vent next to his bed. It sounded like someone whispering. Maybe his parents? He crawled out of bed and got to his knees, putting his ear up to the vent. It was definitely whispering. He held his breath so he could hear it better.

"IT...ITCHES...IT...BURNS...IN THE DARK..." said the whisper. The voice sounded far away, like it was coming through a crackling speaker. The whispered phrase kept repeating.

Jimmy jumped back into his bed and pulled the covers over his head. He shut his eyes tight and hummed to himself so he couldn't hear the whispering. Eventually he fell asleep.

For the next three nights, Jimmy heard the whisper coming from his vent. Each night he had to try to block it out so he could sleep. When he asked his parents about it, his father said he hadn't heard anything, but it was probably the sound of the new pipes, and that Jimmy's imagination was making it sound like words. Jimmy couldn't accept that answer. This was something he would have to solve on his own, but during the day when it was far less frightening.

On the following day, Jimmy unlatched the basement door by himself and carefully stepped down the steep stairs. He pulled on both lights just like his father showed him. He remembered the flashlight he left by the stairs a few days earlier. He checked out the other corners in the basement, swinging the flashlight beam into the shadows. He couldn't find anything out of the ordinary, just some old furniture and his mother's crafting supplies. There was only one place left: the spot under the stairs. He shined the light into the small entrance way. It seemed much bigger inside without his father taking up a lot of space in there, and it was definitely creepier being alone. He blew the fear out of his chest in a short exhale. Crawling in, he held his breath, trying to listen for anything that could sound like the whispering he heard at night. His light went back and forth inside the small area and landed on the dark shape burned into the wood.

Jimmy almost dropped the flashlight in fright as he saw the shape had grown. Not only did it have the shape of a head and shoulders, but there were now arms coming down from the shoulders...and... was it taller than before? Jimmy stared hard at the silhouette, the circle of light wobbling as his hand gripping the flashlight shook. He reached out and touched one of the arms with a trembling finger. It felt hot to the touch, as if it had just burned into the wood. Pulling his hand back with a snap, he reflexively shoved his blistering finger into his mouth and dropped the flashlight in a clatter. The beam of light guttered and then went out. Jimmy frantically tried to find the flashlight, running his hands over the ground, when he heard a voice in the dark. *"IT...ITCHES...IT...BURNS...IN THE DARK. IT...ITCHES...IT...BURNS...IN THE DARK..."* Jimmy reeled back, and forgetting about the flashlight, he crawled for the safety of the basement.

As he scrambled out of the nook, he heard a pop, and the basement light went out. Screaming, Jimmy got up and ran, tripping over the pile of paint cans and twisting his ankle. Tears ran down his cheeks and he could only hobble towards the stairs. As he got to them, the light in the stairwell went out. The only light now was coming from the partially open door of the basement. He heard the sound of the paint cans moving behind him. Something was coming out of the nook. He tried to get up the stairs as quickly as he could, but he could only hop up one at a time, clinging to the railing. Halfway up the stairs, he heard his dad talking to his mother in the kitchen. He started to shout out that he needed help, but his father started the electric saw so there was no hope of being heard. He was almost to the top of the stairs when he saw his mother's hand reach the door to the basement and shut the door. Now Jimmy was in complete darkness. He trembled as he felt something strong grab his arm and a hot breath against his ear.

"IT BURNS IN THE DARK!" screamed the thing from under the stairs as it pulled Jimmy down into the basement.

CLOSET MONSTERS

"Is not!" Lacey yelled.

"Is too!" Anne screamed back.

"Guys, come on. This is silly," Dee stood between the two tweens, ever the peacemaker. This time, it was all because Lacey teased Anne about being afraid of monsters hiding in the closet.

"Whatever, it doesn't matter anyway," Lacey grunted.

"I should never have said anything about the closet, anyway. No one ever believes me," Anne said, her face red from the intensity of the fight.

"Let's go make popcorn and watch a movie—take your minds off it," Dee suggested, hoping the rest of the sleepover would have less arguing and more giggling. It was never like that when it was just Dee and Anne. She knew Anne had a weird imagination and often suffered nightmares, she didn't believe in the closet monster, either, but she'd never fight Anne over it.

"Yeah, okay. Let's go pick a movie. I'll pop the popcorn and meet you in the living room," Anne said as she headed out the door and downstairs.

Lacey started after her, but Dee had another idea. Dee might not have been afraid of closet monsters, but she did enjoy a good prank,

so she crept quietly up to Lacey and gave her a push into the closet with a hefty, "Boo!"

"Oh please," Lacey laughed from inside the closet. "You know I'm not a baby; it's Anne who scares easily. We should lock her in here!"

"I don't think so!" Dee teased, and she slammed the door and wedged the nearby desk chair under the knob to lock her in.

"Okay, Dee, I know you're expecting me to get scared and beg to be let out, but Anne never cleans this closet, so the floor is full of nice, soft, cushy blankets. I could stay here all night," Lacey said. She was cocky, always had been. Dee had always been the patient one, and this time, she decided to let Lacey stay in there until she got the reaction she wanted.

"Dee?" Lacey called from within the closet, relaxed.

"Guess I'll go watch a movie since you're so cozy in there! See ya!" She stomped out of the room and downstairs to find Anne waiting for the microwave to ding.

"You guys pick a movie?" Anne asked.

"Not yet, but nothing scary," Dee suggested.

"I can't sleep after those movies," Anne said.

"I knew you'd say that. I guess we'll just watch musicals all night… again." Dee nudged her as Anne rescued the popcorn from burning and promptly dumped it into a giant bowl.

"You love it, and you know it," Anne said while salting the popcorn, and then, noticing it was just the two of them, "Where's Lacey?"

"Oh, you know how she is, that huge ego. I pushed her into the closet, didn't get a reaction," she shrugged and grabbed a handful of buttery, salty goodness, "so I locked her in."

"You what?" Anne asked, incredulously.

"I locked her in, she's probably asleep already," Dee said through a mouthful.

Anne took off, she ran out of the kitchen, bounded up the stairs, and flew down the hall to her room.

"Wait up!" Dee said, wanting to see if Lacey was freaking out yet.

When Anne got to the door, she jerked the chair out of the way and paused. Dee finally caught up.

"What's your deal, Anne?" Dee asked. She didn't answer.

"Lacey?" Anne asked the closed door.

No response.

Her breath became heavy and panicked, afraid to ask again.

"Lacey?" she whispered.

Nothing.

"Okay, dummy! This isn't funny. You're actually scaring her this time." Dee was annoyed. She walked up to the closet and grabbed the doorknob, but it wouldn't budge. "Lacey Cynthia Bigby, let go! Stop being a jerk!"

Anne covered her face with her hands and said, "It's happening again."

"What are you talking about?" Dee asked, then turned to jiggle the knob. "Lacey! You cut this out right now!" Still no response from her friend and the door remained shut.

There was only silence.

"Oh no... no, no, no, no, no," Anne whimpered, shaking her head and wringing her hands. Her body rocked back and forth. "I should have listened. I never should've let you come here but Lacey was so insistent on having a slumber party here—"

"What are you talking about?" Dee asked, knowing this had gone too far. "We round robin the sleepovers, you knew it was your turn!"

"That's the problem," Anne said. She looked up and stared right into Dee's eyes in such a way that it frightened her.

"What problem?" Dee asked. Anne started to back away.

"I should've made an excuse," Anne said, more to herself than to Dee, "after what happened last time."

"Okay, I get it now," Dee laughed. "You're both in on it. It's not going to work, I'm not scared."

"You don't understand!" Anne wailed. "I was going to wait until you were asleep. Now you'll know everything. It'll take you, too. It was only supposed to be her."

Dee felt her heart beat against the wall of her chest as she turned back to the closed door.

"You stop this right this instant, you hear me in there?" Dee screamed as she beat a fist against the door.

It finally swung open, and Lacey stood deadly still in the doorway with her head tilted down, as though she'd been leaning against it the whole time. Her hair dangled like a curtain blocking her face. Suddenly, her head shot up to reveal empty red eye-sockets and a wide-open mouth, full of gnarly razor teeth.

"What the—" Dee started, but Lacey's hand flew up, and two pencil-sharp fingers darted straight for her eyes. She never even got a scream out.

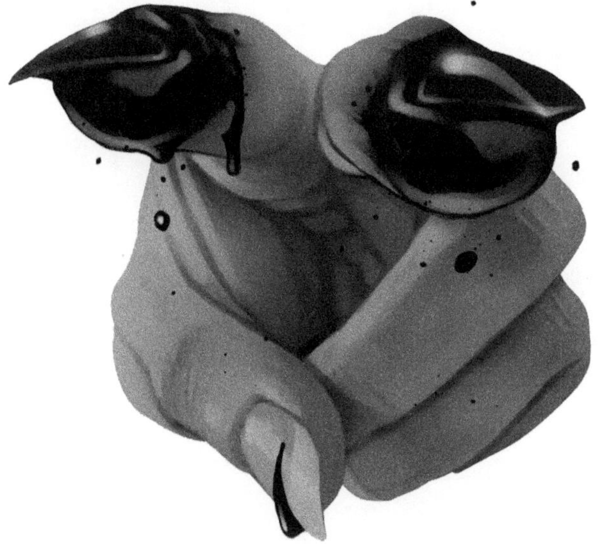

(For extra fun when telling this story, jump with a scream at "It finally
swung open, and—AHHHH!")

THERE'S SOMETHING NOT QUITE RIGHT ABOUT THAT THING

A DRIVING LESSON

Laurie was thrilled with her new car. Her friends' first cars were gray sedans or hand-me-down wooden paneled station wagons, but not Laurie's: hers was a red convertible. Laurie had been saving for two summers for a car, and she finally got one just in time for the new school year to start. It was an older model, from the seventies, but it had low mileage, and it was ridiculously cheap. It had been in an accident, the salesman told her, but everything that had been damaged had been replaced. Laurie didn't care. It was beautiful, and it was hers. She'd have to work extra shifts at the grocery store to afford the insurance, but it was so worth it. Laurie pulled into the student parking lot on the first day of her senior year, with the convertible top down, her sunglasses on, and the breeze blowing through her short dark hair.

After school, she piled as many friends as she could fit into the red convertible and drove up and down the North-South highway through town. She blared the music, and they stopped at three different drive-thrus: one for tacos, one for burgers, and one for sundaes. It was bliss.

That night, Laurie tossed and turned, but she couldn't fall asleep. She attributed it to her excitement about her new ride. When she finally slept, she slipped into a nightmare. In the dream, someone was driving her new convertible. Stolen! Oh, no! she thought. A girl was

driving down a sunny highway in Laurie's car. She was listening to a disco song on the radio, the volume turned all the way up, and her long, straight, platinum hair was blowing behind her in the wind. The girl sang along, steering the wheel with one hand while holding the other into the air and letting her fingers float in the current of wind. The song ended, and an advertisement came on. She started fiddling with the radio. Laurie could see her car drift into the opposite lane. Look out! Laurie cried, and the platinum haired girl put her eyes back on the road to find a truck speeding head-on toward her. She turned the wheel hard. The car skidded and swerved, spinning off toward the guardrail. Laurie's red convertible hit the metal rail and rolled over down the embankment. She could see the twisted body of the car, broken glass, and red blood soaking the girl's blond hair.

In the morning, the horror of the dream had faded. Laurie got ready for school, ate her cereal in front of the TV, and bounced out into another beautiful, sunny day. Today she had to work after school and would get to show off her new car to her coworkers. As she put her key in the door and opened it, the sunlight glinted off of something on the driver's seat. Laurie's heart beat loudly in her ears. She blinked to clear her vision and then looked closer at the seat. Trailing from the headrest was a single long, straight, platinum hair.

GAMESTATION VK

Bret looked down at the open box in disappointment, the tattered festive paper and a ribbon bow tossed to the side. His mamá beamed at him with an open-mouthed smile that showed all of her teeth and the sheer excitement she had from the anticipation of Bret opening this particular gift. The present he thought was the GameStation VR, a virtual reality headset that was very popular that holiday season, turned out to be a stack of sweaters and a week's worth of socks. Bret looked up at Papá to see a look he knew was urging him not to hurt his mama by being ungrateful, so he forced a smile.

The day after Christmas, Bret gathered every penny he could find, but even after adding up the money he got in cards from his grandparents, he still didn't have enough to buy the new game console, not by a long shot. Even with his savings, he was over a hundred dollars short. When he'd taken his old system to trade in at the local game shop, they offered him a measly fifty bucks, in store credit only. Not that it mattered, they were sold out of the coveted new system, anyway.

Bret started doing odd jobs, like shoveling the driveways of his neighbors and picking up groceries for the elderly man who lived down the street, but even after two weeks he was still short the hefty price tag on the GameStation VR. He was seated on the floor in front

of the TV counting it all again, just to make sure. He huffed out a sigh after confirming he still need sixty-seven dollars to buy the headset.

The familiar sound of a certain commercial that had played on repeat since last fall reverberated in the living room. Bret looked up to see kids in futuristic jumpsuits flying around shooting lasers at each other, defying the laws of gravity and joining forces to defeat a giant alien monster until it's revealed that the children were wearing headsets and playing in their living room.

"GameStation VR," a deep, cinematic voice boomed. "So real you'll question reality."

Bret let out a long, deep sigh and let his shoulders hunch forward.

"Papi, why don't you go with Abuela today," Mamá urged after watching her son's face fall. "Help her around the house, go with her to her appointments.

"My abuela used to give me a little cash when I helped her on her errands," Papá said. "I bet she's good for a twenty if you walk her downtown and carry the groceries back."

"The old ladies at the salon pinch my cheeks," Bret grimaced.

"But the old ladies at the salon also have little candies in their purses," Papá said, making a sour face to make his son laugh.

"Okay," Bret agreed, "I'll go for the twenty. Purse candy tastes like perfume and lint, though."

"Fair point," Mamá laughed.

The next day, Bret went downtown with his abuela to help her with a few errands. He handled the rolling cart she always took with her on her walking trips downtown. Once they'd filled the little cart with a few things from the corner store, he went with her to her hair appointment. Once Abuela was seated comfortably awaiting her turn, she opened her purse and handed a few rolled-up bills to Bret.

"Un gustito," she told him. He smiled broadly and shoved the cash in his pocket. Once he had been pinched to the point of having rosy cheeks, he made his way outside with a handful of purse candies that did, indeed, taste a little like lint and regret.

Bret pulled the money from his pocket and unrolled the bill his abuela had given him. He let out a groan.

"Five dollars?" He whined and shoved it back in his pocket with the rest of his savings and looked around for somewhere to kill time while he waited for his abuela.

As he shoved another piece of purse candy in his mouth, Bret noticed a familiar product in the window of a secondhand store just across the street. He ran full speed to the shop with neon signs that proclaimed "Buy, Sell, Trade," "Cash for Gold," and "Electronics." Stopping just long enough to read the price, he quickly knew he had enough. Once inside, he scanned the shop and saw a large man seated in the back corner among the disarray.

"I want that game system in the window!" he called. He ran to the counter, tossed his money down, and that was that.

It wasn't until Bret got home and began to set up the console that he realized there was something off about the label, which read GameStation VK. His face fell. At closer examination, the shiny, black box was barely held together, and he could see the wiring through cracks in the corners. When he looked at the virtual reality headset, he noticed that the soft comfort foam was actually just Styrofoam that had been colored black with a marker and hot glued in place.

He'd been duped.

When he tried calling the shop to ask for a refund, he was greeted by a message stating the owner was on vacation and didn't give a date for his return. Bret put down the phone and stared at the janky knock off he'd spent his hard-earned money on

and grumbled to himself as he plugged it in to charge, deciding he might as well see if it worked.

An hour later, Bret pressed the power button and a tiny light appeared on the headset, which he slipped over his forehead and down across his eyes. It was too large for his head, but before he could adjust the strap, something flashed before his eyes, startling him. Bret tumbled backward and tossed the visor off, letting out a startled yelp. After he'd calmed a bit, he laughed.

"Cool!" Bret smiled excitedly as he stared down at the headset. It might have been a knockoff, but it seemed to work in some way. Maybe the person who had used it before didn't factory reset the system, he thought. So, he turned it off and turned it back on again, just in case.

"'So real you'll question reality,'" Bret said, and he gingerly put the visor back on to see if he could get the game to go to the home screen. As he slid the headset over his eyes, it immediately tightened on its own. Something streaked before his eyes. Bret couldn't make much out, just the shape of something upright with a human-like figure, but much larger and very fast, almost just a blur. He was startled again, and tried to get the visor off, but it wouldn't budge. Fidgeting with it only seemed to make it further tighten around his head. He could see nothing, only blackness.

There was a screech behind him, and he turned his head to barely catch the figure streak out of the way again, but not before it paused for a brief second and Bret saw bulging, yellow eyes and a gaping mouth with rows and rows of large, twisted fangs. Bret reached blindly for the controller in hopes that pressing buttons might release the visor or get him to the home screen. The sound of growling made him frantically turn in circles. He was unable to see anything, but he still heard the growling.

"Okay," Bret said aloud to ground himself, "it's just a game. It's. Just. A. Game." He reached an arm out and felt the edge of the living

room sofa, which helped bring him down from the anxiety a little. His hands shook as he loosened his grip on the controller and turned slowly, still in complete darkness. He relaxed a bit and breathed.

It was at this moment that the thing finally appeared, standing before him, ready to feed. In any other game, Bret knew he could quickly pull a trigger and it would be dead. No amount of button mashing could help him now. The creature's face split in half as the mouth opened wider, displaying more rows of gnarly teeth, its clawed hands ready to tear at him. Bret fell back, trying to remind himself he was still in his living room, and it was all fake, but then he felt the teeth at his forearm. He tried to stand and run, but the monster was on him, devouring him, the visor showing only darkness as he felt each sharp fang sinking in.

When they found the game system on the floor, it appeared as nothing out of the ordinary. Bret was nowhere to be found, not even a drop of his blood left behind.

THE TREE

The tree loomed over her, a leafless canopy of twisted branches disappearing into darkness at the edges of their expanse. Mary approached the trunk, peering into the hollow at its center. She stood on tiptoe, straining to see inside the hole, but couldn't see the bottom.

This is the spot, she thought. He said it would be here. Mary took a deep breath and stuck her arm into the rotten hollow. Her fingertips touched a spongy, wet interior, and bits collected under her fingernails as she blindly searched the cavity. Something crawled over her hand. Mary shuddered, but she continued her quest. You're the only one who can make things right, his voice echoed in her head. Finally, she felt it: a metal chain. She clawed her fingers around it and pulled, yanking her arm out of the cranny.

The gold locket was caked with dirt and decayed tree flesh. Mary used her fingers to wipe away some of the debris. She could almost make out the inscription on the back. She squinted and held the locket closer to her eyes. The letters became a string of looping symbols that Mary could not interpret. Movement in the canopy drew her attention up. She had not felt a breeze, but the branches were swaying as if in a strong wind. She contemplated them, puzzled, and then realized they were not being blown about, but were moving on their own, sliding over each other like a pile of snakes. Yelping in sudden terror, Mary

started to run away from the tree, but the sinuous branches reached down, grabbing at her. They wrapped around her, binding her arms to her sides and her legs together, and then began to lift her up, shoving her face-first into the rotten hollow. Mary screamed and struggled, flailing against her binds. Rotten wood pushed against her nose and mouth, stifling her cries, as the branches tightened and pushed her further inside the tree.

Suddenly, all was still. Mary opened her eyes, and saw the familiar shape of her bedroom window, a slim beam of sunlight framing the drawn shade. She could hear birds chirping outside. "A dream," she sighed with relief. She tried to get up, but she found she could not move her arms and legs. The terror of the dream returned, and bile rose in her throat. She lifted her head from the pillow, craning her neck to see how she was bound to the bed. Her bedsheets were wrapped around her limbs. She kicked and ripped them loose from her legs, angry with her brain for frightening her with such night terrors. She pulled her left hand free and began unwinding the bedding from her right. She found her fingers balled into a tight fist beneath the cocoon of fabric. Mary opened her hand. Sitting on her palm was a gold locket, crusted with bits of rotten tree.

She stared at the oval of gold in her hand, blinking while she closed and opened her hand several times. The locket did not dissolve through her hand, did not disappear like some dream thing. She carefully pried it open and out fell a single large seed. Grasping the seed between her shaking fingers, Mary turned the locket to inspect the inscription. Now she could read the neatly coiled script:

the nightmare has chosen you

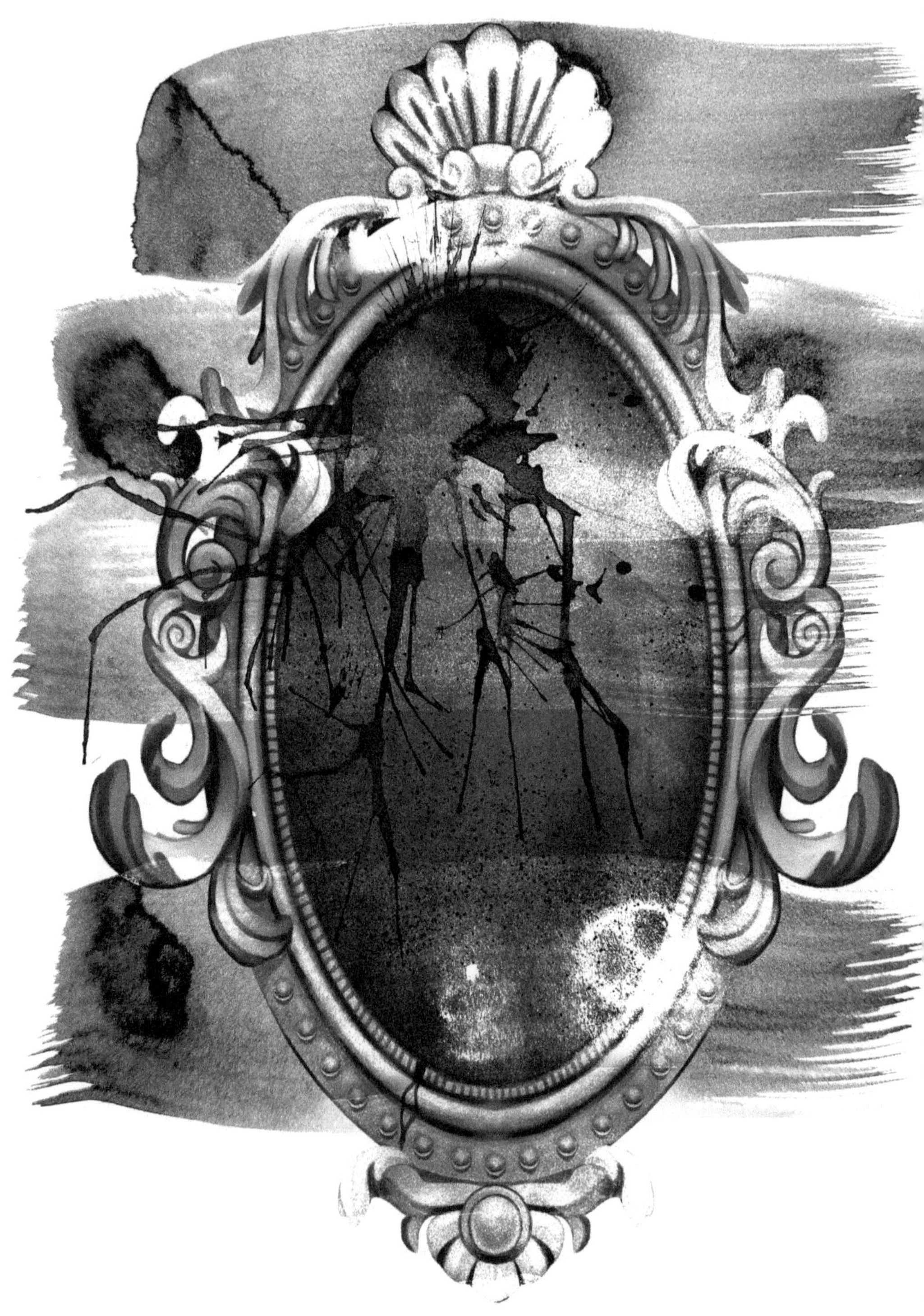

THE REFLECTION

Heidi loved her grandmother but hated her grandmother's house. It was too big and too old, with floorboards that creaked no matter how carefully Heidi stepped, and spider webs draping every ceiling corner. Gran needed a cane for balance and had to traverse the steep stairways up to the bedroom or down to the laundry carefully, placing one foot on a step, joining it with the other foot, pausing to regain her strength, and then repeating the rigid rhythm all-the-way-up or all-the-way-down. Heidi would help her grandmother with chores, like carrying the clothes basket of clean towels to the upstairs linen closet.

In the front hallway, at the base of the main stairwell, there was an old mirror on the wall. It was oval, with roses and cherubs carved into the wood, and the gilding was peeling off to reveal a muddy red undercoat. The reflective silver backing of the mirror had bubbled up from the glass along the top and tarnished black along the bottom. Heidi thought it made her reflection look like she underwater in a dark lagoon, with strands of black tarnish seaweed framing her chin and mysterious creatures looming in the black bubbles around her face. When Heidi walked by the mirror, she averted her eyes, engrossing herself in the lavender scent of the clean laundry, or checking under her fingernails, or staring at the floorboards.

Anything to avoid meeting her own gaze in the strange, reflected version of the old house.

One night in the guest bed, that was too large and too hard, Heidi was reading a book by the dim bedside lamp, and trying not to think about spiders crawling from the ceiling corners and into her mouth while she slept. Suddenly, the light flickered and then went out.

"Heidi, honey," called Gran, "I think we blew a fuse. Be a dear and come here." Heidi went to her grandmother's bedroom door, and Gran handed her a flashlight. "I need you to check the fuse box in the pantry. You know where it is?"

Heidi nodded and plodded toward the staircase. She automatically flicked on the stairwell light switch out of habit, but she was still in the dark. Heidi stood at the top of the stairs for a minute, pleading silently to the electricity to just start flowing. When it didn't, she clutched the flashlight in one hand and the banister in the other, descending the stairs, one creaky board at a time. At the bottom of the stairs, she flicked the switch for the foyer light, pursing her lips in concentration as she willed it to work, but again was left in darkness. She turned back around, heading for the back of the house where the fuse box was. The flashlight caught a strange reflection in the creepy old mirror with the gilt frame: the folds of a white dress on a human form, like someone was standing against the wall opposite the mirror. Heidi swung the flashlight around the room, calling, "Hello?" in a shaky voice. She was alone in the room.

Approaching the mirror, Heidi held her flashlight straight at it, the reflected light brightening the room and filling her eyes. The mirror looked just as wavy, black-spotted, and creepy as usual. No strange white figures to be seen.   Heidi dropped the flashlight beam to the floor with a sigh of relief, then looked again at her reflection in the mirror. She covered her mouth with her hand, clamping in a scream. Looking back at her over the shoulder of her own mirror-distorted

visage was a skeletal face, with stringy black hair attached in clumps to its skull and dripping wet seaweed hanging from its clavicle. A skeletal hand clad in a flowing white sleeve reached out and touched Heidi's shoulder. Heidi didn't wait for what might come next: she turned and bolted out the front door. She loved her grandmother, but she wasn't stepping foot back in that house ever again.

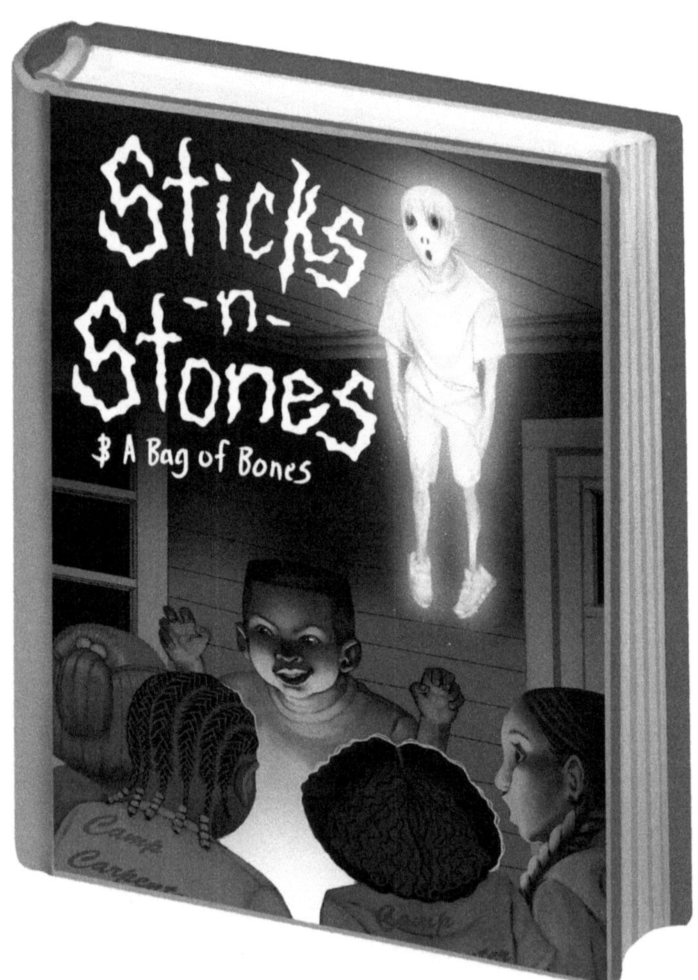

Sticks
-n-
Stones
& A Bag of Bones
Camp
Carver

THE BOOK

During the weekly class visit to the school library, Paul usually sat in the corner of the periodicals section flipping through the pages of a magazine. Sometimes he rolled through slides on the microfiche machine for a while. He never joined his classmates in the fiction section. At the beginning of the school year, Paul had picked the wrong book off one of those shelves, and now he did everything he could to avoid it.

The horrifying book was a collection of short stories. Paul hadn't actually read any of them; he had merely plucked it from the stacks and flipped through it. His thumb stopped on an illustration of a waifish woman with stringy black hair, skeletal features, and empty black sockets where her eyes should be. Every pen stroke of the drawing was nightmare inducing. When he closed his eyes, all he could see was that terrible face. He shoved the book in between its neighbors, imagining one of the horrifying woman's bony hands prying the pages open from the inside and clawing at him. Paul stifled a scream into a shrill squeak and hightailed it to the other side of the library. Out of the corner of his eye he saw movement near that horrible book and turned to see one of the kids from the third-grade class grab it off the shelf. Paul gasped and started to hiss, "Don't!" but covered his mouth with his hand to cut himself off. The third grader smiled

as he looked through the pages, then brought the book up to the librarian to check out it out. Paul felt a little embarrassed. A kid two grades younger than him didn't find the book scary, yet as the kid carried the book past, Paul turned his head away to avoid looking at the cover.

After classes ended for the day, Paul saw that same third grader in the hall ahead of him. Paul stared at the kid's bag; he was sure he could see the outline of the book pressing against the inside. He imagined two dark circles appearing on the fabric, like the woman's black sockets were haunting him through the pages. Paul took an abrupt turn to the water fountain, taking a long drink and splashing some cold water on his face. He lingered by the fountain until he was sure the book had left the building.

A week later, he walked into school to find one of his classmates reading the book. Paul sat at his desk, the book two rows behind him in his classmate's hands, and he desperately tried to ignore the feeling that those eye sockets were watching him. He began to see it more often: a kid reading it at lunch, and another lightly swaying on the swing set, their nose stuck in the book.

In October, the book got passed around between his peers so often that several days he played sick and stayed home from school just to avoid it. It kept Paul up at night, worrying about that skeletal woman's face lurking in a friend's backpack.

In November, their teacher assigned the class to each bring in their favorite book and read aloud an excerpt from it. Paul started to sweat nervously when he saw a classmate approach the front of the room, and he recognized the cover of the book that he had been avoiding all autumn. Paul immediately shot up his hand and asked to go to the restroom. He scuttled down the empty hallway and through the boys' room door, where he hid in a stall. Sitting and humming to himself, he tried to kill the right amount of time to wait out the story.

Ten minutes later, Paul returned to his desk, only to find another student walking to the front of the room with the scary book. "Well!" the teacher exclaimed. "That one is certainly popular. How many more of you chose it as your favorite?" Eleven kids raised their hands. Paul dug his fingernails into the sides of his desk and tried not to scream.

A WORD OF ADVICE

THE GLUTTONOUS THIEF

Walter shoved fistfuls of ripe cherries into his mouth, splitting their sweet flesh with his molars and spitting the pits out rapid-fire, like a Gatling gun, making a target of a broken stump of a fallen tree. Red juices ran down Walter's chin and bloodied his lips. Walter leaned back on a mossy rock, in the perfect hiding place for scarfing his stolen spoils: a hidden, sunny forest glade just off a little-traveled dirt road. He'd nicked the bag of cherries from a farm stand, and he was so pleased with his perfect form on the heist that he'd decided to treat himself by gorging on the fruit.

Chewing away at the last bit of sweet fruit in his mouth, with an arsenal of pits stored safely in his cheek, ready to fire the next spray of ammunition at the stump, Walter heard the rustle of a foot on the ground behind him. He gasped and turned, fearing he'd been caught, and the drawn breath sucked one of the pits to the back of his throat. Walter swallowed the pit.

When he saw who had found his hiding place, he stood, coughing and laughing, an eruption of cherry stones and pink tinged spittle landing at his feet. The offended chipmunk chittered, scolding Walter, and scampered back into the trees. Sitting back down against the rock, Walter finished the bag of cherries. His belly full, and warmed by the afternoon sun, he fell

asleep, chin tucked to his chest, a red berry stain spreading on the front of his shirt.

He woke to a blanket of darkness enveloping him, dulling his senses. A moonless, inky void of sky hung above him, and the forest sounds were barely a whisper of leaves and crickets. The stillness was punctuated with a singular rhythm of terrible pain in his stomach. Ugh. I shouldn't have eaten so many cherries, he thought, but this pain was not like a normal upset from eating too much of a good thing. The pain radiated out of his belly button, like something inside was trying to push its way out. His stomach roiled, and he tried to roll on his side to vomit, but he found he could not move. He flailed and kicked, trying to turn over or get up, but his torso stayed stuck to the ground, like he was rooted to the spot.

* * *

The forest glade just off the old dirt road was a favorite spot for small creatures to gather in early summer. It was sunny and quiet, secluded, with no large predators or humans around. The chipmunks particularly liked to visit the glen, to eat the juicy fruit of the small, lone cherry tree that grew in the middle of the clearing. The chipmunks would climb up the tree, chattering and scolding one another, and chase each other back down its trunk, and then over the bleached white skeleton at its base. They hopped around the skull and ribs and stopped to eat their juicy red snack on the pelvis and legs, before bounding back up the bright red fruited tree right in the middle, growing from the belly of the bones.

THE STARLING

When Albert was naughty in the house, he was sent out into the garden and told not to come back in until suppertime. Exiled, he would look for things to do to pass the time. He liked to catch the sun in his magnifying glass, condensing the light into a hot concentrated beam, and point it at ant hills, watching its occupants curl up and wither into little puffs of smoke. He would capture daddy long-legs off the rough bark of the old oak tree and pull off their limbs until they were just a writhing torso. He would pick daisies and pluck out their petals, not caring if she loved him or loved him not.

One afternoon in the garden, he came upon a nest in a low branch of a laurel bush. There were five small eggs inside. Albert reached into the nest and picked up one of the eggs. It was no bigger than his thumbnail and a pale blue-green color. Albert wondered what color the inside of the egg was, with such a shell. He took the egg to the stone pathway near the shed and threw it at the flat slate. The egg burst open, revealing a bright yellow yolk surrounded by a puddle of clear goo, just like a tiny chicken egg. Albert was frustrated that this egg was so boring, not a tinge of blue inside as he had hoped. But it had made a lovely wet cracking sound as it smacked into the slate, so he grabbed another small blue egg and threw it at the ground in delight. One by one he destroyed the eggs with a satisfying thwack.

As the church bell down the road clanged the hour, Albert left the mess behind and ran inside to wash up before dinner.

In the dining room, Albert found his older sister setting the table. She handed him a pile of silverware. "Make yourself useful," she said, and then went into the linen closet to retrieve the napkins. As she walked back into the room, they were both startled by a loud thump against the window behind Albert.

As he turned to see what had hit it, she said matter-of-factly, "It was a bird. That's a bad sign, you know. It means someone in this house will die soon."

"You think you're so smart. It means no such thing," replied Albert with a sneer, "just that birds are dumb and fly into things."

They finished setting the table, and Albert sat in his usual seat facing the window. He banged his silverware together, drumming up a ruckus, while his sister went to help in the kitchen. There was another loud thwack at the window, and Albert dropped his knife and fork, looking up to see a black feather floating down outside the glass.

"Stupid bird," Albert muttered, and got up to look out the window for the offending creature. A small black bird smacked into the window right in front of Albert's face. He jumped back, startled, but then shuffled forward again to see what had become of it. He saw the little starling fall and land in the bush below the sill. It lay prone, and Albert thought it might be dead, but it roused and took off flying. The bird swung around through the garden, and arced right back at the house, throwing itself at the window again. A small trickle of red blood appeared on the glass as the bird impacted. Albert stepped back, mouth hanging open in disbelief as the bird took flight again and smashed into the window with fury, aiming purposefully at Albert's head.

"It must be dead now," Albert whispered and crept closer to the window. He didn't see the starling in the hedge below.

Suddenly, the pane in front of his face blossomed into an explosion of red, as the starling made her final   crash into the window. The pattern of blood on the glass took on the shape of a human head and torso, with wings spread out on either side. To Albert, it looked like the snow angels he would make in the garden in wintertime, only not white and frozen, but red and dripping: the angel of death. Albert's lip trembled and his eyes began to tear up. He ran into the kitchen, crying, "It's me! It's me! The bird picked me! I'm going to die!"

ELI WAS A DEAD MAN

Eli was a dead man,
Known for the quickest gun.
He tried to fight a rattle snake,
But the rattle snake done won.
He'd hitched a wagon to his ox,
And hit the Oregon Trail,
He wound up in a wooden box,
But still he would not fail.

Eli was a dead man,
And they buried him good and deep.
But you can't stop a dead man,
When the dead man just won't sleep.
In Kansas he was buried,
They left him there to rot,
And the wagon train rolled on,
He was cold, or so they thought.

Eli was a dead man,
But he'd made a solemn vow,
That even if it killed him,
They couldn't keep him down.
Each night they buried Eli,
When they'd stop at supper time,
Each morn his corpse was waitin',
To walk the dusty line.

Eli was a dead man,
But he woke up with the sun,
Walked from Independence,
All the way to Oregon.
Once they got to Baker City,
His kin folk were in luck,
'Cause when they buried Eli,
T'was the funeral that stuck.

Eli was a dead man,
But he knew where he belonged.
He walked the Oregon Trail,
And he walked it good and long.
The day he left Missouri,
Here's what Eli said,
"I'm goin' to Baker City,
Even if I get there dead."

THE NECKLACE

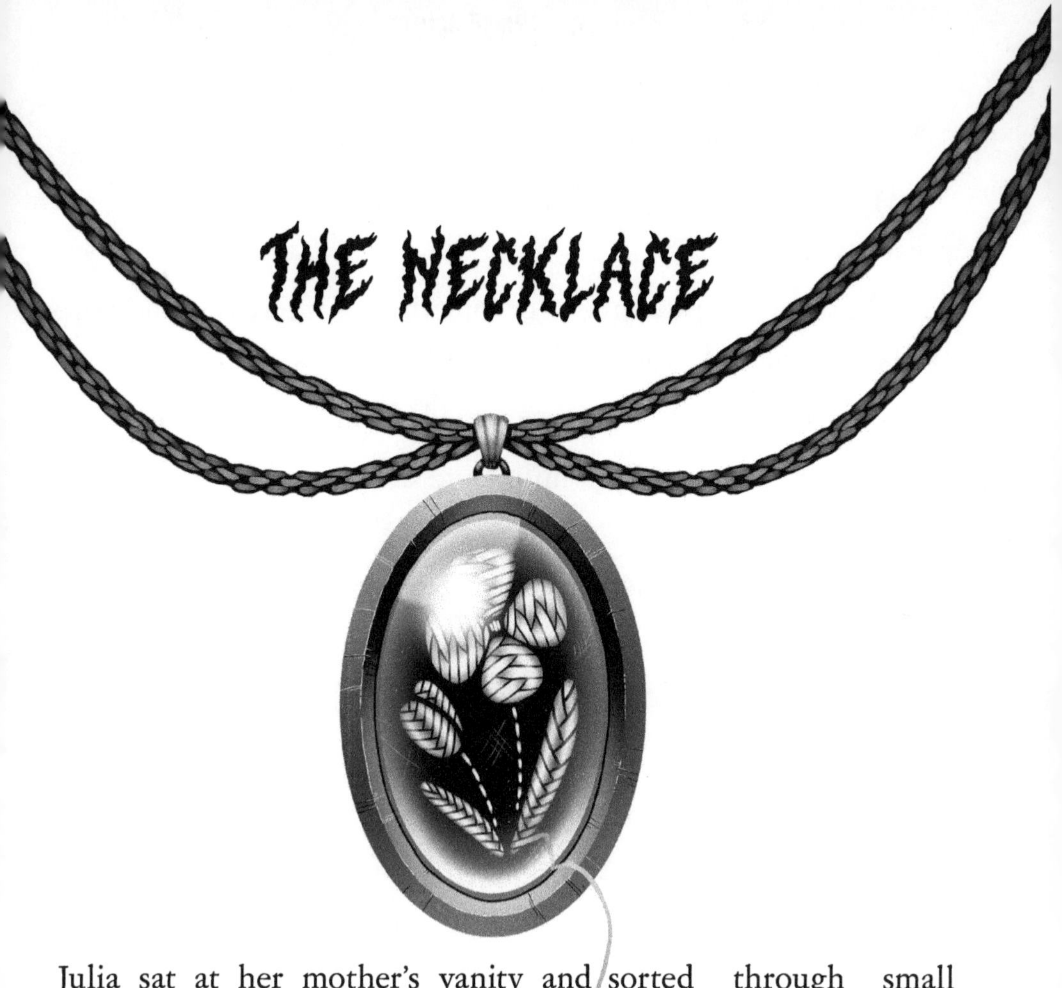

Julia sat at her mother's vanity and sorted through small cardboard boxes full of jewelry. Her mother had told her to find something nice to wear to her cousin's wedding, but there was nothing remotely Julia's taste in the dusty old stuff. There were long strands of yellowed pearls, giant clip-on earrings studded with rhinestones, and an enameled broach that looked like Bambi. Among the bobbles, Julia found one necklace that was at least wearable. It was a small oval pendant, with a domed piece of glass over a tiny, intricate bouquet of flowers embroidered in gold thread. Kind of cute and Boho, Julia thought as she clasped it around her neck.

She went down to the kitchen to eat her breakfast. As she sat, spooning cereal into her mouth, her mother noticed the necklace.

"I'm surprised you chose that one," she said.

"It was the only half decent one," Julia replied.

"That necklace is special. It's mourning jewelry from your great-great grandmother."

"Like she wore it at a funeral or something?" Julia asked and slurped the last of the milk from the bottom of her bowl.

"No, it's a memento mori: it was made from her hair after she died."

Julia coughed and spit milk out, dripping over her chin and down her dress.

"Mom! That is disgusting! Why would you keep this thing?!"

"Mourning jewelry was common in Victorian—"

"Ugh! Spare me the history lesson. No way I'm wearing it."

"You don't have to wear it, but you do have to treat it with care. We need to wipe it down and put it back in its box."

Julia's mother reached to remove the necklace, but Julia pulled away with annoyance. "I can do it myself. I need to put on a whole new outfit now anyway, thanks so much for that, Mom," Julia replied, rolling her eyes and pushing past her mother out into the hall.

Julia stomped up to her room to change into something that wasn't milk sodden. She looked down in disgust at the golden hair flowers, with drops of milk spattered on the glass. Unclasping the chain, she went to the corner of the room and tossed it inside a trunk filled with her old toys.

After an afternoon of overcooked banquet chicken, wedding cake with frosting that tasted like it was ninety percent shortening, and way too many old people attempting to do the Electric Slide, Julia escaped back up to her room. What a waste of a day, trapped with relatives, she thought. Attempting to evade the outdated moves happening on the dance floor, Julia had been abruptly encircled in a

very bosomy hug by Great Aunt Sophie and subjected to a litany of stories about family members who were gone long before her mother was even born—more history lessons she didn't need or want. Julia flopped down on her bed and sighed.

Out of the corner of her eye, she noticed a curl of yellow hair hanging from the lip of the old trunk. A doll's hair must have gotten caught when she'd closed it earlier. She got up to stick the stupid toy's mane back inside. As Julia cracked the lid, more hair began to pour from the edges of the trunk. Golden strands cascaded to the floor, covering Julia's feet. The locks flowed out in all directions from the center of the trunk, where one of Julia's old dolls, with a cracked temple and staring out of only one unblinking blue eye, smiled at her angelically. Around the doll's neck was the mourning necklace. Julia stepped back in horror, but the hair had wrapped around her ankles. Her balance lost, she fell on her back. She lay dazed and felt the strange tickle of the hair as it crept up her side.

A soft voice whispered in her ear, "Memento mori. Remember death."

Blurred images drifted into Julia's mind and slowly came into focus.

A woman with features like Julia's mother, yet dressed for a different age, in a bustled dress and an elaborate hat with her hair swept up inside it, and a few escaped blond curls framing her temples. A small child in a long white dress clutches one of the woman's gloved hands.

The same familiar woman, propped on pillows in a bed, cheeks gaunt, blood-spattered handkerchief pressed to her mouth, while the child, older now, sits bedside, holding the woman's thin hand.

The child, a woman herself now, stands before a marker stone carved with "Mother" in elaborate script, her hand on the chain of the necklace at her throat: a small oval pendant, with a domed piece of glass over a tiny, intricate bouquet of golden flowers.

Julia opened her eyes. She propped herself up on the floor with her elbows and looked at the trunk. The lid was open, but the cascade of hair was gone. Julia crawled forward on her hands and knees just enough to see over the lip of the trunk, and found a jumble of her old toys, the yellow-haired doll on top of the pile, one blue eye looking right at her. Atop the doll's chest, gently cradled in the folds of its white dress, was the necklace. Julia carefully picked up the chain and looked closely at the little flowers, at her great-great grandmother's hair arranged in a tiny bouquet.

"I understand," she whispered. "I'll remember" to the tiny blooms resting in her shaking palm. She wiped the glass dome clean on her shirt, stood, walked to her mother's room, and returned the memento to the safety of its box.

HOLD YOUR BREATH

Julie drew in a long breath and held it. Rachel, in the passenger seat, mistook the inhale as an exhaled sigh, and looked over at Julie.

"What's wrong?" she asked. Julie, lips pursed shut, raised her right hand off of the steering wheel and held up her index finger. Rachel stared at her with concern.

"What are you doing?"

Julie exhaled loudly as they passed on to the block after Saint Michael's.

"Were you holding your breath?" asked Rachel.

"Yeah. Why didn't you? Always hold your breath as you drive past a cemetery. You know."

"No, I don't know. What kind of nonsense is that?"

"My grandfather taught me to do it when I was a little kid."

"Ok, so your granddad was sick of you chattering non-stop and a made up a game to keep you quiet in the car."

"No. It was to keep me safe. If there was a body buried recently, its spirit could be trying to escape, and if you breathe it in, it could get stuck inside of you," said Julia earnestly.

Rachel burst out laughing, covering her mouth with one hand and slapping her knee with the other.

"Whew… Sorry, Julie, but that is truly ridiculous. Do you hold your breath walking past a cemetery, too? Or at a funeral? You'll end up a permanent resident if you black out and fall in the grave!"

Julie simmered. "Just drop it."

Rachel continued, "You picked the wrong route home. We're going to pass Saint Joseph's, too! You better start conditioning your lungs."

"I should have just let you walk," Julia irritably retorted.

Rachel sighed. "Ok, I'm sorry. I was just poking fun. It is a weird thing to do."

Julie responded with silence. As they approached Saint Joseph's Cemetery, out of habit, she sucked in a bit of extra air and held it.   Rachel, however, smiled wickedly, quickly rolled down the window, and stuck her head out. Julie slapped at Rachel's arm as Rachel leaned further out of the window. Rachel took comically exaggerated gulps of cemetery air. As the two of them rolled past in Julie's car, a group of people dressed in black and gathered around a grave turned quizzical eyes upon the teenage girl hanging out of the window, breathing loudly and smacking her lips with a contented, "Ahh."

Julie was mortified as she noticed the mourners, and clawed at her friend. Rachel popped her head back in the window and rolled it up. They passed the cemetery wall, and Julie expelled stale air and took an exasperated breath, filling her lungs.

"I can't believe you did that! Those poor people! That was a funeral!"

"Oh, it's fine. Now they'll have a funny story to tell. Also, nothing happened to me, so now you have proof that you can quit your silly superstition."

"I know you were just 'being funny' or whatever, but this time you took it too far, Rach. That was not cool."

Julie drove on in silence, and Rachel began fiddling with the radio. She scanned the FM stations, past several songs that Julie knew Rachel liked, and then pressed the AM button. She finally settled on a station playing something orchestral, with a smooth male voice singing, "Til the end of time…" Rachel began to sway slightly side to side.

"Do you know this song?"

Rachel's voice sounded a little strange to Julie; it seemed to have a slower cadence than moments before.

"I've never heard it."

"This one came out when I was in high school."

Julia took her eyes off the road and glanced at her friend in bewilderment.

"What are you talking about? We are in high school, and I've never heard this song."

Rachel ignored Julie's confusion, saying, "I just love Perry Como," and began to hum along.

"Are you kidding me? Sounds like something my grandfather would listen to."

"Perry is such a dreamboat, I simply must play you this album."

Pulling up to a stop sign, Julie held her foot on the brake while she turned and looked fully at her friend. "Ok, Rachel, I know you're messing with me. Cut it out." She waited for that wicked grin to appear on Rachel's face, signaling the "gotcha!" moment of her prank.

Instead, Rachel gazed at Julie with a dreamy look in her eyes and asked in that same slow cadence, "Before we go home, can we stop at the malt shop? I have a hankering for an egg cream."

Julie was certain there hadn't been a malt shop in town for at least 50 years.

THE PHOTO ALBUM

"What's that?" asked Amber's roommate, leaning against the door frame of their shared bedroom.

"My family photo album," Amber replied, flipping slowly through the pages of the large leather-bound tome. She lingered on some of her favorite shots. One from before Amber was born of an unidentified toddler, covered in mud and beaming proudly. Her third birthday party, with Amber sitting in her grandmother's lap, present unwrapping in progress. Her cousin's graduation party, a shot of the whole family standing in a group under a makeshift awning of a giant blue tarp, muddy puddles visible in the background. Last Christmas, with Grandma in her favorite doily-adorned floral print armchair. One more: the final picture of her grandmother, from a few weeks ago.

"Are there pictures of you as a kid? Can I see?" her roommate asked with a smile as she took a step toward Amber's bed. Amber closed the book.

"I'd rather not…"

"Still too sad?"

"Yeah," Amber replied, looking at the photo album in her lap.

Her roommate nodded and disappeared into the common area. Amber crossed her legs on the squeaky dorm bed and sighed. It was true, she was sad, but her stronger desire was to avoid judgement from a house full of women that she barely knew. It was hard enough moving away to school and trying to make new friends in her new life, but leaving for three weeks halfway through her first semester had put a larger rift between Amber and her roommates. They had bonded while she was away burying Grandma and cleaning out fifty years' worth of memories from her grandmother's house. Now the three of them seemed like fast friends, and she was basically a stranger. She could hear their shared laughter echo down the hall from the common room. There was no way her roommates would understand the photo album.

* * *

When Amber was young, she thought her family's tradition was something that everyone did. At parties, her uncle would set up his camera on a tripod, call the family to pose together, and then quickly run and join the group as the timer ticked down. "Smile!" he'd call, breathlessly, taking his position in frame as the camera flashed. They did the same after Easter Mass, weddings, and christenings. At the age of seven, at her first wake, Amber saw her uncle setting up his tripod. The family gathered around Great Aunt Sadie in her casket, and took a family photo. This time, her uncle didn't tell everyone to smile, but Amber did anyway.

A couple of years later, she showed a grade school friend the family album. The friend was mostly disinterested, but laughed when she saw a photo of Amber with cake on her face and frosting in her hair, from her first birthday. She flipped through the pages, and then stopped, saucer eyed, at the one of Aunt Sadie and the family.

"Is that a dead person?" whispered the girl in disbelief.

"That's my Gran's oldest sister," Amber replied.

"Who takes a picture with someone in a coffin? And why are you smiling?!"

Amber twisted her face and blinked in confusion at her friend's outrage.

"We always take family photos when we're all together,"Amber said, pulling the album toward her and examining the photo with newfound scrutiny.

"Not at funerals! No one does that."

"They don't?"

"What's wrong with you? You're twisted!"

Her words rang in Amber's ears. Something was wrong with her family.

At Great Uncle George's wake, teenage Amber saw the tripod set up and her stomach burbled with unease. She slipped away and hid in the coat room when the family gathered around the casket. Later, her mother was furious that Amber had missed the group photo.

"My poor uncle," she lamented. "How can he rest knowing his grandniece didn't honor his memory?"

"Taking pictures of dead bodies is weird, Mom! It's embarrassing, and I'm not doing it anymore."

"That's not just some body," her mother replied, "That is a man that loved you–loved us."

Amber let out an exasperated sigh and stormed off, slamming her bedroom door with adolescent outrage. Why couldn't her family just be normal?

Years later, Amber arrived to her grandmother's wake fresh from the bus depot, feeling disoriented. As much as she wanted the independence and chance to prove herself, moving away to college and

far from her family support system had been harder than she thought. She felt pulled between both places: worried about the classes she'd be missing and how she would catch up, and fretting that she had not been there for her grandmother at the end. As she approached the casket, she saw her Grandma's careworn and stoic face, and all of the good memories of the older woman flipped through her mind, like the pages of the family album. She sat next to her mother in the viewing room and leaned her cheek against her mother's shoulder. The loss of her grandmother felt like a small hole in her chest, and she couldn't imagine how big the void was in Mom's heart now that her own mother was gone. When her uncle set up his tripod, Amber stood right next to the casket, and put her hand on top of her grandmother's. As the camera flashed, Amber smiled through her tears.

* * *

Sitting back on her pillows on the squeaky dorm bed, Amber opened the photo album and turned to the last photo. She scanned the sullen faces and then stopped at her own smiling visage. She noticed another smile in the group, one that she hadn't before. In place of the peaceful but stern look she vividly remembered on her grandmother laid to rest, she now saw a warm, closed-lipped smile. A tear rolled down Amber's face.

What a weird tradition, she thought, and a special one.

Amber slid the album under her arm and headed toward the common room with resolution. "Hey," she called to her roommates. "I have something to show you."

SNAKE OIL

Molly was dripping with jealousy. Kimmy had perfect hair, luminous skin, and easy popularity. Kimmy was Molly's cousin, but the two had also been best friends up until middle school, when Kimmy discovered makeup and pom poms. Molly, on the other hand, thought herself far too plain. She watched as Kimmy curled her hair into perfect, dark spirals that fell about her shoulders as she got ready to go to another party Molly hadn't been invited to. Both girls stared into the large mirror in the bathroom at Kimmy's. Molly kept trying to emulate the way Kimmy had contoured her makeup but mostly ended up just looking like she forgot to wash her face after a camping trip. Kimmy noticed and frowned.

"Don't worry, babe," Kimmy said. "You'll get better at it the more you do it!" She set down her curler and unplugged it before spraying her curls with a mist of hairspray. She held a makeup wipe out to her cousin.

"That bad, huh?" Molly asked grumpily.

"You look like you fell asleep babysitting your little brother while he was playing with markers," Kimmy laughed.

"I'm not going," Molly said into the makeup wipe as she scrubbed her face.

"Oh, don't be so dramatic," Kimmy said.

"I wasn't invited anyway," Molly stared at her face in the mirror, back to normal, back to basic.

"Suit yourself, babe," Kimmy glossed her lips and made a kissing face at Molly in the mirror. "Stay here and be miserable by yourself again. Another Friday night alone all because you're too afraid to just be yourself."

"That was harsh, Kimmy," Molly said as her cousin breezed by to grab her jacket.

"Just accept that this is how you look, you'll be happier," Kimmy said.

Molly couldn't accept it.

It was for this reason that she was easily persuaded to spend her entire allowance on a product that was guaranteed to change her life. Molly often spent her weekends wandering the mall, but hadn't noticed the little kiosk, or the middle-aged blonde woman with the thick, unusual accent, before. Perhaps it was because it was a new fixture in the mall, or maybe it was the strange location, down a deserted hallway of the shopping center, where several businesses had closed earlier that year. She occasionally went down that hallway to use the restrooms, which were cleaner than the ones in the more populated areas of the mall or at the food court. There was a church in what used to be a department store that was only open on Sundays, and several kiosks. Most were empty, but there were a few that only opened sporadically, and one farther down that did cell phone repairs where a bored looking middle-aged guy sat watching videos on his tablet.

As Molly passed a kiosk lined with little jars, the woman standing at it exclaimed, "Lovely cheekbones!" At first, she thought the woman was talking to someone else, but there was no one else but the two of

them and the guy with the tablet a little farther down. He'd looked up briefly but went back to whatever he was watching when he saw where the sound was coming from. The woman rushed around the kiosk to get a closer look at Molly, who was astounded by the attention, but she enjoyed the way the woman cooed and took her hand, leading her to a stool.

"So very pretty!" The woman's eyes examined Molly closely, making her feel like she was under a microscope.

"Excuse me, I was just going to the—" The woman shushed Molly and rattled off a few things so quickly that one could hardly make out more than half a sentence here and there. Molly caught "a makeover" and "free today for you" and "won't take no for an answer."

"Such lips!" the woman said. "I will enhance with this!" She held up a tube of liquid that was a deep red. Before Molly could protest, the woman was painting Molly's lips. "And now the eyes," she went on, holding up a palette of eyeshadows in varied tones. Then there was an eyebrow pencil, a small brush, then a larger one, then a huge one to set it all with a soft powder that smelled of lavender and chalk.

While the woman worked, she talked on and on, but Molly was overwhelmed and distracted by the feeling of the makeup going onto her skin, the smells, and the sound of the woman speaking in circles. Molly decided to just let it happen and gazed at the various containers lining the cart. There were bottles, jars, tubes, and containers of powders. She saw perfumes and makeup brushes for sale, and a hundred different things attractively arranged into a large carrying case with a $500 price tag that had been crossed out. Below it, handwritten, it said $399. Kimmy's stomach turned at the number, knowing she could never afford that. It was a good thing the woman had said "free today for you" or she would've been in big trouble.

Kimmy had tried to do Molly's makeup a few times but gave up because of the way Molly groaned throughout. This time, she couldn't

see the process and had no idea what colors the woman at the kiosk was using or if it looked good or bad, and she spoke so quickly that Molly couldn't interject even if she wanted to.

Molly gasped when the woman handed her a mirror, for the face staring back at her no longer appeared plain—it seemed to take on her cousin's features. Sure, they both had blue eyes and black hair, and there had always been a subtle family resemblance, but not so striking as it was then. There was something more subtle, the way her lips curled into a slightly different smile from Molly's own, or the way her eyes seemed to hold a mischievous secret. Somehow, the woman at that kiosk had captured the elements in Molly that shone so brightly in Kimmy's face with only the use of makeup. Even her eyebrows seemed rounded exactly the way Kimmy's were, even though Molly's had always come to a point at the middle. It was uncanny, and for a moment it felt like an out-of-body experience staring into that face that both was and was not Molly's.

"How did you—" Molly began, but the woman cut her off.

"It's what you wanted, no? Beauty?"

"Yes, but how—" Molly was, again, cut off.

"It's amazing what a little mag—makeup can do," she smiled slyly.

"How much?" Molly asked.

"One hundred. A small price for perfection."

"I don't have enough," Molly lamented as she stood to leave.

"Only seventy for the eye makeup, come back for the lipstick later," the woman urged.

"No thanks, I—"

"May I show you one more thing?" The woman asked, holding up a black jar. Molly knew she couldn't afford it, but if the woman was going to somehow make her prettier, she was willing to listen.

"This is a very special cream made from rare botanicals and oil from snake venom." Molly cringed at the mention of snakes, the woman continued, "Old family recipe. It will strip away everything you hate about yourself. You will never need makeup again." Her voice was ominous, but before she knew what she was doing, Molly had forked over fifty dollars for the magical jar.

That night, after she'd washed away the shiny lip color and smoky eyeshadow, Molly sat before her vanity. It was strange after spending the afternoon glancing in mirrors and seeing someone so different and then suddenly turning back into her old self. She immediately reached for the jar the woman had sold her.

The directions were in another language she didn't recognize, but the saleswoman had said to apply it each night. Molly scooped out a bit of the cream, which tingled and even stung slightly. The woman said the venom might have this effect, but Molly knew the benefits would be worth it, so she began to rub it on her cheeks. She soon realized that her skin was turning red as she smeared the substance into her skin.

Molly thought if she just waited it out the burning would go away, but the longer it was on her face the more painful it became. Involuntary tears welled up in Molly's eyes and she knew that she

needed to wash it off right away. By the time she reached the bathroom her face was on fire, and her eyes were so swollen that she couldn't see. She splashed water on her skin hoping for relief, but none came. After trying in vain to soothe her skin a while longer, Molly realized she could see again. As she lifted her chin, she saw herself in the mirror and screamed. Her eyelids and lips had melted away to reveal the stark white of teeth and bone underneath. Her skin became a slow waterfall, like wax dripping away from a candle that had burned too long. Her left eye purged from her skull as acidic bubbles tore at the rest of Molly's forehead and cheeks.

* * *

The saleswoman looked at the clock and glanced back at herself in the mirror, waiting for change to appear on her face. Finally, after hours of waiting and watching, her cheekbones seemed to lift and the tiny crow's feet disappeared at the corner of her eyes, which appeared to be turning blue. Her skin became taut and supple, like that of a much younger woman; even her subtle age spots were disappearing. She shook her straight, blonde hair, which had become a rich black by the time she stopped the motion. She smiled at the stranger in the mirror and said, "Beautiful."

STICKS N STONES

"Say it again and I'll put your lights out, ya hear me, new kid?" Pete huffed, his right arm pulled back.

"Sticks," the new kid paused to spit out a tooth, "and stones!" Pete slammed his fist right into the new kid's left eye.

"I'll show you sticks and stones!" Spittle flew out of his mouth as he growled down at the kid whose only crime was being new and responding to the town bully with something his dad told him to say.

"That's what I thought, no fight in ya, nothin' but a kitten." Pete clutched the kid's collar. "Say meow, kitten."

The new kid spit blood out but didn't respond.

"Say meow, little kitty!" Pete held his fist at the boy's chin. Still nothing. Pete rolled the new kid over on his stomach and pulled his arm back. "Meow, wittle kitty!"

"Owwww!" the new kid groaned.

"Say meow, wittle kitty!" Pete pulled harder.

"Okay, meow, meow! Please stop!" the new kid cried out.

"Say it like a poor, wittle kitten." Pete pulled on the arm again.

"Oooowwww! Meow!" he mewed between screeches of pain.

"Remember this next time you talk back to Pete McNay, got it, kitty-boy?" Pete released him and the new kid was up and running. Pete laughed and brushed the red hair back from his forehead as he turned to walked down Chestnut Street. He rounded the corner onto Pickering Street and, on approaching a well-known brick wall, crossed to the other side, knowing he didn't want to run into Gilda, the Crazy Cat Lady of Pickering Street.

"Young man!" he knew her crackled voice, having heard Gilda yelling for her many cats to come for dinner each day. He sped up and kept his eyes to the ground.

"Can you help me?" she hollered from the gate. He glanced to where she stood on the sidewalk behind her vintage station wagon.

"It'll just take a moment; I need help with these bags of cat food," Gilda called to him. He walked faster. "Peter McNay, you rotten boy!"

Suddenly he changed his mind and crossed to her, almost as though there was a sudden pull urging him to go to her. Several old cats were perched on the wall watching his approach. Gilda wore an unkempt gray dress with a rainbow of patches sewn over the many holes scattered across it. Her cheeks drooped and, with her bushy gray eyebrows, the old woman seemed to have a perpetual scowl on her wrinkled face. Her salt-and-pepper hair was a matted mess, as though birds nested in it when no one was looking. Pete gave her a once-over, from the dirty scarf on her head to her unmatched boots, one of which had a hole so big you could see three toes. Two cats rubbed up against her ankles, awaiting a meal. Pete laughed at the look of her.

"Come to help me after all?" she asked.

Pete sneered at her and grabbed one of several huge bags of cat food. At first, he'd thought maybe she would give him a few bucks for the work, but he didn't like her tone, so he tossed the armful right onto the sidewalk with a thud. It split open, and kibble spilled out in a waterfall, drawing all the nearby felines to come and feast.

"Look at what you've done, you terrible child!" She was disgusted.

"Sticks 'n stones!" Pete snarled, mocking both Gilda and the boy he'd beaten to a pulp. He turned his nose up as he walked away.

"Yes, that's right, boy, sticks and stones…" she said, her voice low and deep like an ominous recitation. Pete stopped, his feet were suddenly stuck to the sidewalk. Something shifted in the air, like the morning mist rolling in, but isolated to the little strip of Pickering Street where they stood. The eyes of the many cats turned to Pete, and they began to slink toward him.

"What the—" He tried to move his legs but couldn't. Pete wasn't afraid of small animals, but there was something sinister in their eyes, a blackness that hadn't been there before. Fear crept over him as he looked over his shoulder, "What are you doing?"

She sent in her army of cats, "Get him, my darlings."

The animals swarmed, scratching and gnawing at him, clawing their way up his legs and body, tearing at his clothes. Between screams, he heard her voice chanting:

"STICKS AND STONES,

AND OLD CAT BONES.

ROTTEN CHILDREN,

A ROTTEN SEED SOWN.

PETER MCNAY,

LEARNS HIS LESSON TODAY.

A CAT HE BECOMES,

A CAT HE WILL STAY."

The drove of felines tumbled to the ground and scurried away, leaving one small, orange cat, curled up on a pile of shredded clothing. Startled, the cat leapt up and backed away, hissing at Gilda and arching his back. The other cats had scattered, and Gilda knelt and held out a hand, opening it to reveal a handful of strange herbs. The orange cat began to relax a little, drawn by the scent of the dried green leaves in Gilda's weathered palm. As the cat came closer, his fur settled and his stance loosened. At first, he pulled back when she reached out to pet him, but the herbs drew him closer, irresistible. Now, he would serve her forever.

THE MARBLE GARDEN

There was a graveyard,
In old Salem-town,
Where flowers grew wild,
And grew all around.

They grew on the path,
And on all the graves,
They even sprung up,
On all the pathways.

There were Bluebells and Aster,
and Devil's Paintbrush,
Deadnettle and Daisies,
Bleeding Hearts, pink and lush.

Haymaids and Lillies,
All covered in dew,
And in one little corner,
The Moonflower grew.

John the gravedigger,
Couldn't keep up,
Though each day a bouquet,
For his wife he did pluck.

He picked Ghostpipes and Nightcaps,
And white Widow's Frill,
And Black-Eyed Susan's,
For his brown-eyed girl.

But John never picked,
From the Moonflowers, blue,
They could bring death,
This, the gravedigger knew.

His love often begged,
For the pretty blooms,
But he told her, "My love,
They're the flower of doom."

So she sighed and settled,
For the blossoms he'd bring,
Until she grew ill,
and she asked for one thing.

"John, my darling,
a final request.
Let me hold a Moonflower
When I greet Death."

The gravedigger loved her,
He couldn't deny,
the one thing she wanted,
Before she would die.

So he gathered each bud,
With extreme love and care,
But the poison was strong,
And it mixed with the air.

As he breathed in the blight,
He knew his own fate,
For the Angel of Death,
Stood at the gate.

"Please, they're for my love,"
John gave his last breath,
"Let me bring them to her,
T'was a final request."

And before he'd finished,
Death stepped aside,
His love stood behind him,
And he knew she had died.

The Moonflower sealed,
The gravedigger's fate.
Lost his wife and his life,
For a lovely bouquet.

In the old marble garden,
Together they'd be,
Buried 'neath the Moonflowers,
For eternity.

THE CAMPFIRE

MONSTER HUNT

We're so glad we found you, we need your help! You've journeyed a long way through the pages of this book, maybe you can help us. You see, we've been tracking a horrible monster for a while now, but we've lost it. It must be hiding somewhere within these stories. It's a terrible thing, I hate to ask you because once you've seen it, well, you'll never be able to forget. That kind of thing changes a person. You seem smart, and so brave to have made it this far. Maybe you can help us decipher the last clue so we can find and trap the monster once and for all? What do you say? Here's the clue we found:

46/4/2/5

95/6/5/9

24/4/3/15

158/2/1/10

103/2/3/4

67/2/2/1

If you need help, we can try and figure it out together on the next page—or if you think you've got it on your own, flip the book check for the answer on the next page .

Clue 1: What could these numbers mean? How do they work together? Maybe the answer isn't on this page— what if the first number is directing us to a different page? But then what are the other numbers for?

Clue 2: Page... then maybe paragraph? And after that?

Clue 3: Maybe it could be telling us what line to look at. What is the last number for?

Clue 4: Word! It has to be page/paragraph/line/word, I'm sure of it

How to Solve: The clues are structured page/paragraph/line/ word. Each line of the code leads you to a specific word that will reveal the location of the monster.

Answer:

The Monster Is In The Closet

CREATE YOUR OWN CLOSET MONSTER

<u>FREESTYLE YOUR OWN MONSTER OR USE A SIX SIDED DIE TO LET FATE DECIDE</u>

WHAT COLOR IS YOUR MONSTER?

1. GREEN
2. RED
3. PINK
4. BLACK
5. BLUE
6. ORANGE

WHAT IS YOUR MONSTER MADE OF?

1. FUR
2. SCALES
3. SLIME
4. PLANTS
5. SKIN
6. BONES

HOW MANY EYES DOES IT HAVE?

1. NONE
2. EIGHT
3. ONE
4. SIX
5. THREE
6. TWO

HOW MANY LIMBS DOES IT HAVE?

1. FOUR
2. TWO
3. SIX
4. EIGHT
5. ONE
6. NONE

WHAT DEFINING FEATURES DOES IT HAVE? ROLL THE DIE TWICE (OR MORE IF YOU DARE)

1. SHARP TEETH
2. HORNS
3. TAIL
4. FANGS
5. EXPOSED BONES
6. STITCHES

1. CLAWS
2. TUFTS OF HAIR
3. BANDAGES
4. SPIKES
5. PLANT GROWTH
6. BUG INFESTATION

<u>NOW DRAW YOUR NEWLY CREATED CREATURE INSIDE THE CLOSET</u>

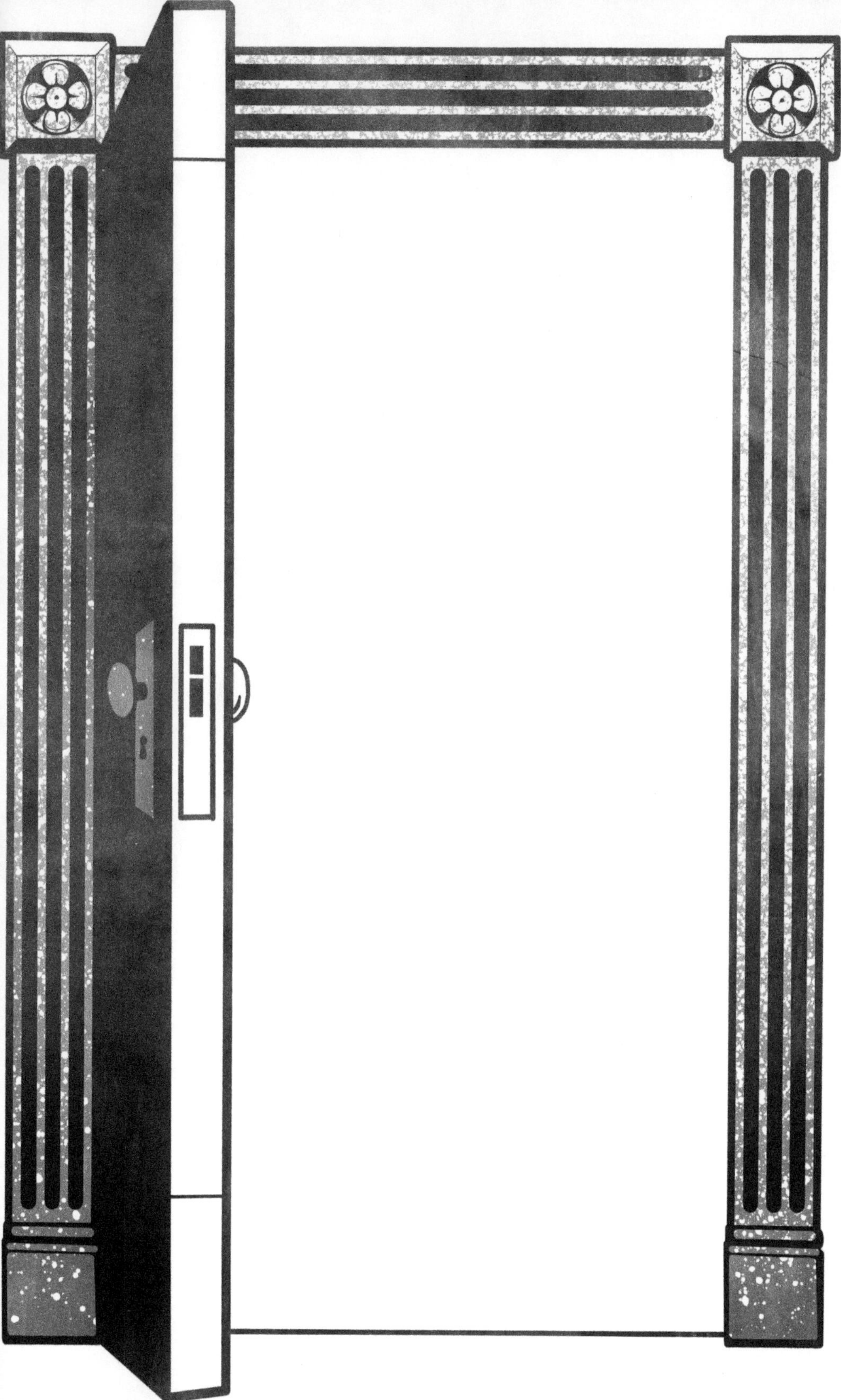

COLOR AND CONNECT THE DOTS

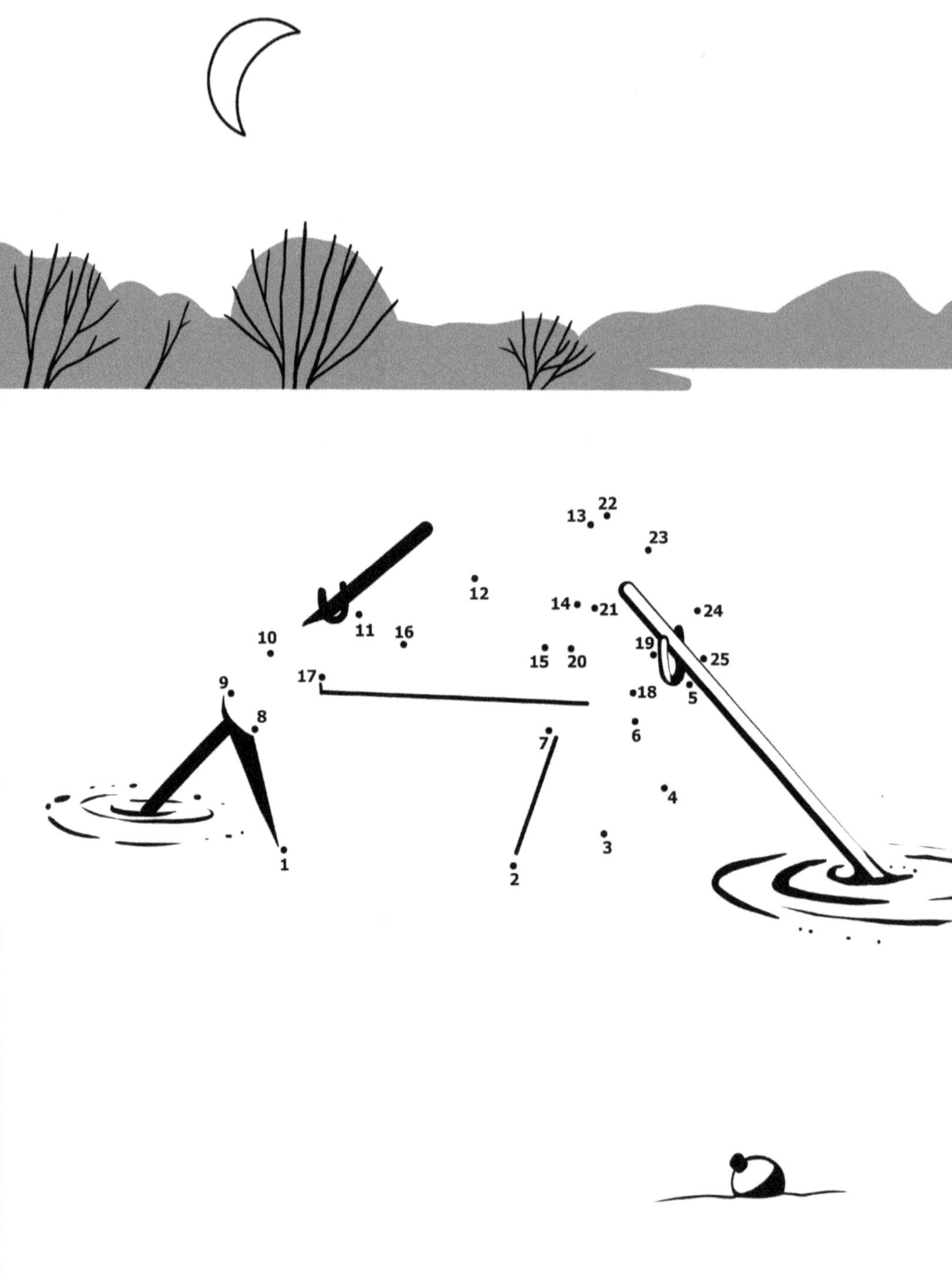

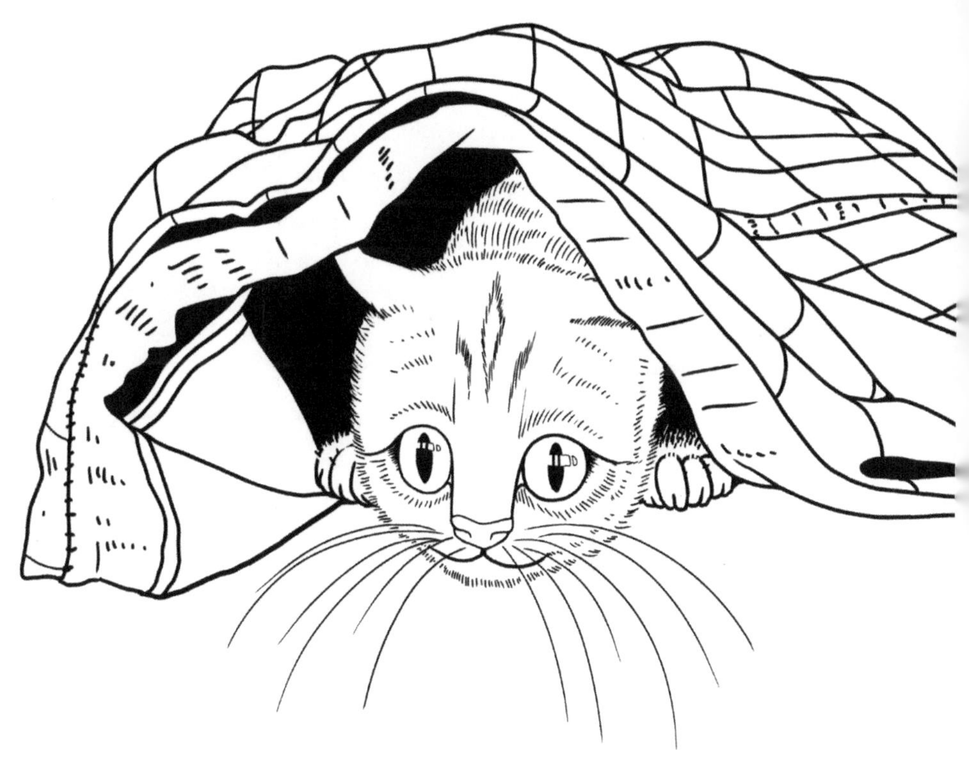

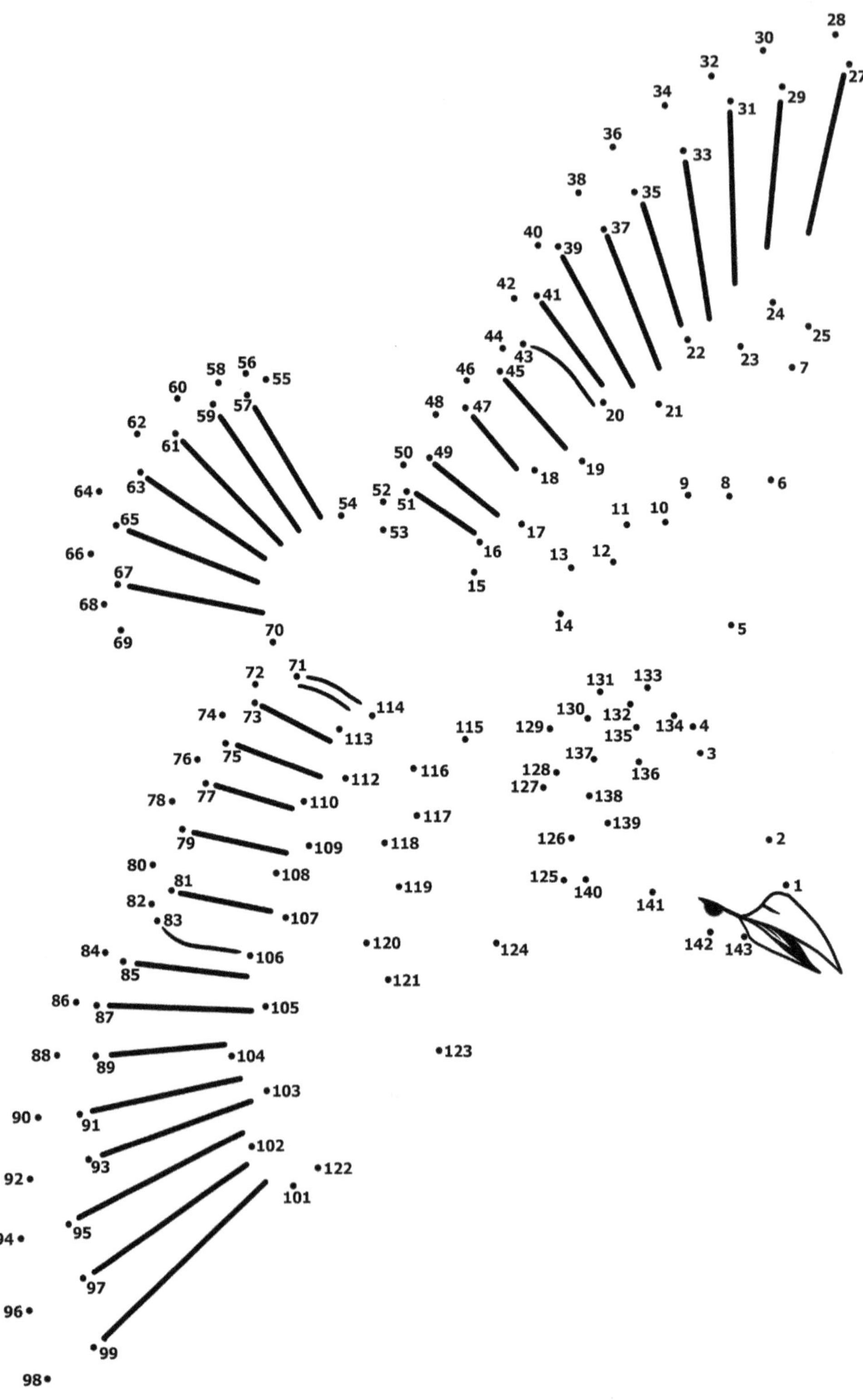

Camp
Camp